WHISPERS

OF THE OFFICE WIFE

Anything is possible.

A NOVEL BY

Mary Ann Gamble

For information regarding permission, please write to:
info@barringerpublishing.com
Barringer Publishing, Naples, Florida
www.barringerpublishing.com

Design and layout by Linda S. Duider
Cape Coral, Florida

ISBN: 978-1-954396-49-4
Library of Congress Cataloging-in-Publication Data
Whispers of the Office Wife / Gamble

Printed in U.S.A.

Dedication

Where there is chaos, there is calm,
Where there is arrogance, there is humility,
Where there is greed, there is generosity,
Where there is egotism, there is modesty.

C.

There is a fine line that is often crossed. You will view the personality of a loving, caring, and warm-hearted individual. Then, you wonder. Is this generosity? Is there an ulterior motive? Why is he/she doing this for me? Then, another being appears—shrewd, cunning, manipulative, and power-driven. Here we go, jump on the roller-coaster ride of your life! The lure of this exciting ride attracts many but only a few hang on tight and know when to swerve and posture both your physical and mental awareness. It's quite a skill to acquire and the reward is the thrill!

I know; I have experienced all the emotions of this ride. There are joys and benevolent generosity of wonderful clients, along with nights of fear and tears, the doubt of my abilities, and searching for the strength to move forward. It's all a part of this world!

You see, administrative support is a grueling, 24/7 position that can wear you down if you let it. BUT there is some incredible magic that happens.

I dedicate this book to **all** support staff in corporate, non-profit, and independent companies. Each of you hold a unique position. The talents and gifts you bring to your job can change the morale and profits of the company and your own future. I also dedicate this book to all women who are faced with challenges and tragedy. At some point in our life, we all must hold our head high and move forward. Let this book be your guide and inspiration to know you are enough and there is not a thing or a person that can stand in your way of finding your authentic self!

Start weaving a beautiful tapestry with vibrant colors of your contributions, your compensations, your joys, and your challenges. You can create your dream job. You can create a life beyond your wildest dreams. You can make a difference! My tapestry is stitched with the threads of my work for employers, friends made along the way, and lessons learned.

I also dedicate this book to each of my employers and clients. Each relationship was not only a life lesson, but also a stepping stone in building my success in business and personal growth. I was gifted beautiful vacations, jewelry, musical concerts, and meet and greet events to honor the "rich and famous" but most of all I was gifted with experiences. Experiences that formed my world and allowed me the freedom to express my authentic self. That is a gift!

I offer tips and tactics after each real-life account! They are tried and true and will make a difference in your professional and personal life. There is a treasure chest at the end of each chapter holding a gemstone that will reflect the story's lesson. Collect them all!

Go ahead, create YOUR beautiful, colorful tapestry.

Create Your Life!

Introduction

Do you want to know a Secret?
Do you promise not to tell?

Listen to my whispers.

Come closer. Hush . . .

Some of us remember the old TV game show *I've Got A Secret*. Panelists tried to guess something about the contestant that is amazing, embarrassing, unusual or just the "secret." Curiosity provoked the win! EVERY person has a secret. From the time of Adam and Eve, the secret has prevailed as an intriguing mystery that promises forbidden truths.

The Beatles top hit "Do You Want To Know A Secret?" compels you to immediately take interest and you promise not to tell! Your lips are sealed!

Come closer . . .

I have the secret tales and the astonishing truths of the '*Office Wife*.'

There is a saying; "no one knows what goes on behind closed doors." Well, I am here to tell you <u>exactly</u> what goes on behind those doors! Yesterday, today, and tomorrow.

I have known the secrets for many years. It is time for me to share the unbelievable, hysterical, insane, incredible, and sometimes very abusive "behind the doors" life.

My purpose for writing the secrets of the office wife is two-fold. One is to share the unimaginable life behind the scenes of the golden gates, the flash and cash, the ego, insanity, and generosity. My encounters reveal the true humanness of every person despite their wealth, power, or prominence. Your curiosity will be fulfilled!

The second purpose of this book is to coach and guide you with tips and tactics from my *Treasure Chest of Gems* to successfully climb the administrative scale, reveal your authentic self and through your experiences—weave your own tapestry with the colorful strands of knowledge, wisdom, experiences. It is YOUR time to be the best you can be!

How This Office Wife Was Conceived

My story is based on real experiences I encountered in the high-profile administrative world. My involvement as an Executive/Personal Assistant to the "rich & famous" was beyond my wildest dreams. I jumped into unchartered waters, swallowed a lot of water, treaded when needed, and learned every stroke I needed to stay above the water—no sinking allowed!

In 1995, I ended a twenty-year marriage. He was the love of my life.

I thought it was the worst thing that could happen to me, even though I knew I was unhappy and tried to ignore the red flags. I often had nightmares that one day I would not be married to this man. I cried through the night and was so happy to wake up and know it was just a dream! I felt the death of my marriage would be the epitome of tragedy.

I was a naive young lady and knew nothing of our finances. As many wives in that era, the husband handled all the affairs. My name was not even on the checkbook. I had no credit cards in my name, nor on the deed of the house. I had zero credit and no understanding of how to handle finances. Back then, most decisions were made by my husband. I never doubted this was the way it was with every couple. It seemed to work! I fell into the depths of the loss of my identity and the pattern of *The Stepford Wives.*

Once the divorce process ended, I thought my life was over—alone and financially, mentally, and physically broken. I felt guilt, sadness, heartbreak and depression. Over the years, I learned how to keep peace in the marriage and the home. As we all know, through experience, every divorce holds terrible tales of pain and hurt. He did this, she did that. He said, she said. The purpose of this book is not to expose my personal divorce drama . . . this is not a memoir! The purpose of this book is to illustrate the path I took to reach my fullest potential and create a new prosperous, fun, peaceful life using my past as a plus and focus on what I *did* know and what I *would* do to move forward in a positive, healthy life. This is possible at any age, at any time in your life. You can change your world!

When you look in the mirror, who do you see? If you are in disguise and accepting anything other than what serves you, it is time to realign your life. When I looked in the mirror, I knew the face staring back was not the authentic Mary Ann Gamble. That face, hair, smile, laugh was totally not me.

A dear friend of mine, Leo, knew I was in a state of loss and depression. He mentioned there was an upcoming women's retreat called "Women of Courage." He did not encourage me to attend— he forced me to go! I did not want to go at all. I did not think for one second it would help me. I tried to play the "poor" card. That didn't work, he already paid my registration fee. He drove me there. Leo was a large scary looking dude! He had been in/out of prison for years for various crimes. He was now sober and an active Alcoholics Anonymous member. You just knew NOT to argue with Leo! He had a heart of gold and cared about me like a sister.

So there I was . . . at this women's healing retreat. Most of the women were members of AA or NA. Some just lost a loved one through death or divorce. All carried loss and sadness in their hearts. I didn't think I fit in. I was better, so I thought. Ha! I fit in perfectly. I was the same.

The retreat's agenda included daily meditations, hikes, yoga, drum circles with several "New Age" speakers. One day, I was sitting in on one of the healing lectures and the speaker asked us to do a visualization exercise/experiment. She asked us to close our eyes, and all was still. Next she said, "Imagine your authentic self walking down the street towards you. Picture how she looks, how she walks, what she is wearing, how her hair is styled, her facial expression, her smell—the real "you" walking towards "you" today. Would your authentic self recognize you?"

That was a deep awakening for me! The vision permeated my entire being! That moment changed my life. My authentic self and the "me" on that day were two different beings. I cried so hard and so loud, I had no control of my emotions. The speaker took me by the hand and led me to a large sitting rock on the trail and told me to sit in solitude for a while. I did not move.

I knew that profound moment changed my life. I was awakened and determined to self-heal and unveil my truth.

What I didn't know was the years of working in the schools and the twenty years of my marriage would soon be turned into lessons that served me professionally.

My first step was to run away! Now that doesn't sound like the best advice, does it? We cannot run away from our problems, but we can change the mood. I flew off to the beaches of southern Florida. I did not know how healing the waves of the ocean, the sunrises and sunsets, putting your feet in the sand, and totally immersing yourself in nature would heal my soul, mind and body. This was my saving grace. I inhaled every moment of healing!

Reality set in, and with zero bank accounts, I had to find a job!

My career to this point was in education. For fifteen years, I was the school secretary to the principal. I loved the kids in the school, and many found comfort coming to my desk and talking about sports, home life, friends, studies, etc. I enjoyed each one of them. I knew intuitively that they needed to share their little stories and grab a piece of candy off my desk! To know what others need is a gift not to be ignored. Another tactic acquired through marriage.

We all have our little secrets, our hidden truths. Some are damaging to our person, and some have proven to be the keys to unlock our future.

In this book, I have gratefully included the perks, the generosity, and the amazing people I met along this path that included first-class travel, spa days, meeting the Hollywood stars, basking in a health resort in Baja, California, jewelry, and multiple well-earned "gifts" of the trade! The names and locations have been changed to respect their anonymity. Some of the stories in this book are shocking, some are very sad, some are very entertaining and humorous. They are all true. Secrets revealed and lessons learned. I decided to write this book to share the entertaining stories I experienced in this different world of secrets, money, and ego.

But that was not my ultimate goal. My wish for this book is to fall into the hands of not only administrative support professionals but any person who is not feeling "enough" or not living their authentic life, who holds pain in their hearts, and settles for what they believe is all they can be and their dreams are just dreams. Use this as a guide to know how to maneuver your professional life and your personal life into the ultimate experience that allows you to be you, explore the vastness of opportunities, and enjoy a peaceful, balanced life.

Stand firm in your own beliefs and boundaries, and there will never be a man or woman who will intimidate you. I had the sense to step back, watch, listen and act accordingly. I took nothing personally. Holding my head high, I moved forward and never told anyone what was going on behind *my* closed doors. Confidentiality is key.

I am confident you will learn the tactics to release and uncork your full potential. Once you learn the techniques to secure the job of your dreams that allows freedom, financial security and the opportunity to transform your life from "hopes" to reality, you will feel empowered.

MARY ANN GAMBLE

Chapter One

Exclusive Limited Offering—You!

"Always do your best."

The Four Agreements by Don Miguel Ruiz

Have you ever sold anything? Maybe you placed an ad on eBay, Etsy, or Facebook Marketplace. Those are exceptional sites to attract buyers who are searching for furniture, rental property, household goods, etc.

If you have placed an ad, you know the first step is to take a clearly focused, brilliantly enhanced picture of your object. You are sure the angle is right, and the object is enhanced to its finest beauty. Next, you write a brief description of how wonderfully this product has served you and entice the buyer to think that *this is quite a deal and I better buy it now*!

Remember, YOU are the product. When you are looking for a position that is in alignment with your skills and talents, and your intuition tells you this would be a great match—go for it! I offer you the key to that magical position!

"I love to interview!" Said, no one! It is stressful, fearful, and surely you will lose a night's sleep before the appointment. That, we believe, is part of the process to secure the position of your dreams! It does not need to be that way at all! Most interviews start with the HR Director. If you make it past that gate, your next interview will be the CEO/President/Owner. Today, virtual interviews are the norm. You only have to make a professional appearance from the waist up. Years ago, you had to buy a suit, heels, stockings, be sure your hair and makeup were perfect and physically interview at the office.

The *Diamond Gem* in this chapter will remove the fears and tears of the "interview." Here's my story. . . .

When I relocated (ran away from home), I needed to find employment ASAP. As I mentioned previously, my divorce left me penniless. I filed for bankruptcy. My gift was FREEDOM! I was on my own, with no money, no husband, no boss, and the reality of being single. Time to recreate my life at 43 years old, whatever that involved . . . I had no clue!

I answered multiple "Help Wanted" ads from the newspaper as this was 1996! I answered a post for a Legal Assistant. I am not, never was, and never will be a Legal Assistant, however, I needed to practice interviewing. It had been fifteen years since my last interview.

And here begins my journey.

I was called to schedule an appointment to interview as a Legal Assistant. Yes! I had no idea what I would say when they asked me about my legal background. I just figured I would wing it! I arrived promptly at 8 a.m. at this beautiful beachfront office. The entrance door to the suite was not inviting at all. There was no business name—just the suite number. My adrenalin was pushing me to open this door, only to find the reception area was even less inviting.

I was greeted by the image likeness of Alan Harper right out of *Two and a Half Men*. Totally awkward, he welcomed me to take a seat in the small waiting area that held four chairs, one table and a lamp. Not even a magazine! Within ten minutes, another applicant arrived. Five minutes after that, another applicant arrived. Alan Harper greeted each one with the same monotone, mysterious welcome. We started to chat, and we were all there for an 8 a.m. appointment for different positions. *Interesting.*

At 10:30 a.m. *yes,* two hours later, I was called into the back office. I never saw anyone come in, other than the applicants. 'Alan Harper' called me to follow him to the back office. I realized there must have been a back entrance for the CEO. I followed his lead and walked into the back office—a large dark room with a desk, no files and there were two men in the office. One huge man was standing next to the desk where the other man in the room sat at a gigantic desk, staring at a piece of paper. The one standing was the size and shape of a refrigerator! The one seated was a younger gentleman, dark hair, head down reading my resume, black turtleneck, black wool blazer. I questioned that right away! Why is he dressed in all black, it's an August, hot, steamy day in a tropical climate? Suddenly, in a gruff, flat voice he said, "Sit down." I felt a strange vibe, almost fearful, weird. I did not know who this man was, what he did, or why he was so arrogant. I was about to find out. This *character* pops up in other chapters!

I did not sit down. Now, I felt mistreated and a little bit angry. I just stood there. I felt this was so wrong and strange. I remained standing and I reached out my hand and blurted words I didn't plan on saying! "Excuse me, sir. Good morning. I'm Mary Ann Gamble." I reached out my hand for a handshake. He looked up and saw I was standing, and my hand outstretched for a shake. He started to acknowledge my hand, and I raised it higher—stand up dude! He stood up, barely looked at me, but did shake my hand! And he spoke! In a low grumble, I heard "I'm David. Let's get this going, I have a lot to interview!" Seriously? "I have been waiting for over 90 minutes for you. I could have gone on another interview and been hired already!" He was silent. His "bodyguard" was staring right through me. It was a quick 10-minute interview, mostly asking me ridiculous questions—so unprofessional and random. He shook his head, let out a huge sigh and offered me $30k. What? Mentally I'm a mess, thinking well at least you will have a job. Again, somehow, someway, my mouth uttered words that came from an inner voice of self-esteem. "No, $62,000 is the least I will accept." He finally looked right at me and laughed! "You were only a school secretary." I let silence speak. He asked me why I thought I was worth $62,000. I sold the product! I let him know exactly why. "I believe, just from this interview, that working for you will be quite challenging and time-consuming. I have the ability and the stamina, not to mention my administrative and personal assistance qualifications. $62,000 is the fair salary for this position." He laughed again! Two laughs in one interview! "OK, Mary Ann, you start Monday. Come to this office every day at 9:00 a.m. I will call you later in the day and tell you what I need." I had no clue about the job duties involved or nature of his business. The old saying "fake it till you make it" worked. I got a job! And I sold my product, as weak as it really was—my intent to honor myself with integrity and value won.

The position with "David" was a long, two-year challenge! More on that drama, and the crazy life of this millionaire in the other chapters.

Honoring yourself and knowing anything is possible is weaved throughout this entire book with a story and a lesson. This chapter focuses on *YOU—the PRODUCT.*

This two-year position was a constant cry for me to do my best and be my best! And it was a great asset as a challenging experience for my resume! On to the next . . .

Nothing lasts forever! Back to the head-hunter! Within a week, I had two great interviews. One position was Executive/Personal Assistant to a world-renowned golfer. He had many outstanding entities all over the world. I found out during the interview that his wife was the top gun. There was the catch! He could not keep an assistant because of the wife's rude, demanding, and demeaning attitude toward every Executive/Personal Assistant. That would be a challenge. I heard through the grapevine that this was the challenge in this position. Power-driven, ruthless wives can be more difficult than a power-driven, ruthless man because jealousy shows her ugly head. The salary was great. It was a suit/heels position. Majestic offices. I was thrilled to have the interview. His CEO escorted me into his magnificent office. There he was! Bigger than life! And, much more handsome in person than on TV. Being a golfer, I was in awe of this man and his accomplishments! The interview went well. He was charming, funny, sincere, and gorgeous! He welcomed me to sit and taste his award-winning wines. I told him, "Probably not a good idea right now as it is 10 a.m. and I'm interviewing!" He laughed and said, "good answer." He also asked me if I played golf. I said, "not as good as you!" More laughter and a totally relaxed, professional interview. The CEO sat there very stiff and robot-style. No expression. Looking very cautious. I felt good about the interview and left with a smile and confidence. Later that day, I learned the reality of this position—his demanding wife would be my boss. This overshadowed the gorgeous man and office! I was told I would receive a call back in a day or two for a second interview. My intuition was not as accepting and excited. The still small voice in me yelled *"RUN!"* I was offered the position. That afternoon, I informed the employment agency the glorious golfer job was not a fit for me. When it sounds too good to be true . . . it probably is. I knew better!

The next day, the employment agency called to offer an interview with the CEO/Founder of a large manufacturing firm in the high-end business district. There was no initial interview with the HR Director, because there was no HR Director!

I was informed the employer was a well-known guru in his field. He authored many books, knew tons of high-profile celebrities. He worked out of a residential office condo complex. The condo was not his residence, but somehow, he finagled with the management and they allowed a corporate lease. She said it was like no other office I had ever worked in! She was spot on! She described the office as furnished with couches, a desk, and fully-stocked kitchen. It was a T-shirt, flip-flops, and shorts position. The salary was comparable to the previous interview. The atmosphere was very relaxed. The interview was not as relaxing. It was a group interview. If you never attended a group interview, picture a police lineup! There were four other candidates. Each scheduled for the 9:00 a.m. interview slot. One by one, the same question was asked of each of us. A total of seven questions were fired at the squad! Talk about pressure!

My appointment was at 9:00 a.m. in his office. I arrived at 8:45 a.m., and he answered the door and let me in. Picture a tall, lanky man, balding with a few sparce, well-placed curls. Running shorts that were too short, a runner's shirt with stains and sweat. Big smile, loud, bellowing welcome to his *"humble abode."* Now this was different! Quite charming office/condo. A little kitchen stocked with tea pot, coffee pot, cannister set, exactly as my dear headhunter said, it was like someone's home! The living room had a beautiful leather couch, and a huge dining table was his desk. The décor overflowed with comical statues, gag gifts, humorous art—fun!

The employment agency described him perfectly as quirky, unconventional, and kind of strange. Sounds like the perfect challenge.

My welcome was overwhelming. He offered me a seat at his desk—the large round dining room table and gave me a bottle of water. He seemed charming. I never had the CEO offer me a bottle of water in an interview! This was different. He said others were joining us. At that moment, I saw a flash of "Lurch" from *The Addams Family*!

Over the next fifteen minutes, six other girls arrived at the office. They, too, were interviewing for the position of Executive/Personal Assistant to this CEO. He invited all in, gave each a bottle of water, and the round-table interview began.

He introduced himself as "Mr. Nice N' Easy." He asked us each to introduce ourselves using just our first name. He then let us all know we were each competing for the same position. The interview process was not an ordinary interview! He started by asking a question "Why are you here?" to each one individually. How stressful is that? You listened to each girl's response and when it was your turn, you were hoping and praying you said the right thing—which, in turn, means it was better than the other's. This is when confidence in who you are pops in strong! Good question, "Why are you here?" My reply, "to secure this job!" So now, I knew I had to prove it!

This round-table interview was intense. I watched each lady squirm with each question, sweat on the brow and the deep swallow. The interview was conducted in an intimidating, mocking, uncomfortable manner. One by one, they would fumble with an answer, nervously clenching their sweaty hands together and trying so hard not to look intimidated. Eventually, the most honest of the pack got up and left! That set the tone for the others who knew they were not equipped to work for this off-the-wall man! He dismissed two of the candidates after an hour. The sweat on their foreheads was a neon light of fear! The look of relief when he released each one was priceless. *Free Again*!

One of the candidates was my assistant, Rita, in my previous position. She was shocked to see me applying for the same position. I was so happy to see her again. The interview continued with me and my former assistant. Three more questions for each of us. I was proud of Rita, she held her own. She presented well, was beautifully dressed, and polished (that's why I hired her).

He asked Rita the final question, "Why should I pick you?" Rita looked at me and smiled, hesitated for a moment, then found her strength. "I am more than capable of fulfilling all the needs for this position. I have read all your books and admire your work and business etiquette. My experience is vast, and I have acquired the knowledge and expertise to office manage and assist you in the highest-level Executive/Personal Assistant capacity." Sounded great! He smiled, flashed an eyebrow raise at me, and applauded her reply. Her interview ended, and she was escorted out. He let her know he would call her later that afternoon.

I was the only one left. He asked me, "Should I hire you or the other girl," not knowing she was my former assistant. I smiled and asked him if he had ever read her resume? Clearly, he did not. (As I later found out, he never read much. He had his assistant read articles and write a synopsis for him. I did that daily for years). "Of course, I did," was his lame reply. Ha! I don't think so! I asked him if he remembered seeing my name as Rita's direct manager at another company, the same company on my resume.

He was not thrilled with me! No smile. His facial expressions changed. He looked at me like *I was the challenge* and was heading to battle! He fired the last question. "Why should I pick you?" This is when I knew I had to "shine" with my true self. Having confidence and knowing I am selling a product—me! My answer (with a smile), "Love the question—'why should I pick you?' You have read my resume, you already know my qualifications are top-notch, you know why you should pick me. Let's put it this way, would you rather have me or my previous assistant as your Executive/Personal Assistant? It really is your choice to decide which level of assistance you are seeking. Who will give you your money's worth?" I ended with a smile and confidence. There it is! Simple. He picked me.

His final comment to me, "You will never have to wear that suit again." Bingo! Got the job and started working right at that moment. Shorts, T-shirts, and flip-flops were relaxed attire, but don't let that fool you. The position was anything but relaxed!

Treasure Chest Gem: The Diamond

Remember, diamonds are a girl's best friend! YOU are the product. Sell it with confidence. You know your strengths. Focus with faith. Believe in yourself. Do not be egotistical and haughty. Be you. Be your best you.

An interview is not much different than shopping. Every store owner is polishing their product. You are the store owner of your qualifications: your knowledge and why you are interviewing. The consumer looks over each item and decides what is best for them. In all truth, the item that shines and is crafted with quality materials is pleasing to the eye, presents well, and stands out among the rest always wins!

You have everything in your possession to shine. Sell, knowing the quality of YOU!

You are your own salesperson.

MARY ANN GAMBLE

Chapter Two

There's A Kind of Hush

"There are limits to the amount
of information one can share.
Confidentiality is essential."

—Gijs de Vries

Embrace confidentiality in all matters. You will know a whole lot of secrets behind the scenes! You will be privy to the most confidential and personal matters. You will overhear conversations as well as be part of conversations of the utmost confidentiality. Respect "Silence is golden."

Who is this funky, crazy ole dude? How does he get away with saying whatever he wants to say to whomever crosses his path? How does he get away with intimidating every wife, girlfriend, colleague? And, why oh why, does he come into work with a clown suit on? He challenges every employee, waitress and still holds his head high and will bellow out a laugh you can hear across the county? In spirit, he is just a little boy playing the game of life. He has a heart of gold and will give you all he has. He is an ego-driven author, who quite frankly had a ghost writer for all his books. He is not a mean man. Everyone loves him. Eccentric would be a mild description. I immediately thought of Red Skelton! Bright red/orange hair, tall and lanky! He always wore the most expensive popular men's cologne. For years, he wore Old Spice, and then the world of expensive cologne became his passion. As an indulgent, exaggerated man, he wore way too much! He was a typical old man with the fancy, red Ferrari. He had a wonderful sense of humor and was quite a jokester. He loved—absolutely adored—toys and playing tricks on people. Gimmicks of all sorts! He collected crazy objects of art. It was not unusual for him to walk in the office around 8:30 a.m., singing loudly and dressed in a costume of some sort, or totally soaked with sweat because he ran from his home to the office. He is a man you never forget! Rodney Wentworth. He was known to his colleagues, friends, and family as "The Rodster." Everyone who lived in his world had their own opinion of the Rodster.

I was the Executive/Personal Assistant/Office Wife to the Rodster. Our office was a residential condominium turned into a business suite. We cooked lunch in the kitchen, played music all day and at 3:00 p.m. it was happy hour! On cue, all employees were drinking some wine, vodka or beer and snacks! The living room served as our main "Boardroom." This is where the action took place! Executives/Entrepreneurs from all over the world came here for at two or three day sessions and listened intently to this masterful man sell his goods! They would pay a minimum of $10,000 for the session. Rodney had no notes, no handouts, no pamphlets to offer. He just talked and they listened and inhaled his every word. I watched the groups of high-profile, successful men respect this crazy character, love his charisma, and absorb his quirky tips and tactics.

The walls were adorned with selfies and photographs of him, movie stars, athletes, political figures, and CEOs of Fortune 500 companies. This was "Rodney Wentworth World" patterned after Dolly Parton World! The difference, we all knew some of the movie stars were photoshopped in! That was the beauty of this man. He got away with it, and we all knew his secret. I knew secrets beyond this façade!

Rodney Wentworth was a personality all his own. He was old-school: paper and pencil, handwritten calendar. Eventually, he ventured into using an iPhone, and was never the same again!

He was bigger than life walking down the enchanting streets in the prestigious neighborhoods of the *rich hood*. In a restaurant, he would walk by a table and comment to others about their food. "Yummy, yummy! Look at what you have to eat!" Once, he even reached and pulled a strawberry off a lady's plate and smiled and said, "thank you!" The customer was shocked and laughed. Rodney had an extendable fork that he purchased on a gag gift online site. That was his humor! That fork went with him to every restaurant. It was quite amusing to watch the expressions of people when he would reach out with his fork and take a piece of food off their plate! Who does this? Only Rodney. Today, he probably is still shocking the crowds, and they still love it, I am sure.

His love relationships with women were not the storybook romance. Rather, as you would guess, they were spontaneous, wild, and he pursued young, arm candy. He loved blondes, tall or short, big boobs, and a sense of humor. During courting, there was a pile of cash and gifts to adorn his precious new young lady. During the courting stages and beyond, he was filled with distrust, insecurity, and dark jealousy.

He was recently divorced, again, when he met Norah. Norah was a lovely, young, naïve, mother of a ten-year-old shy boy, and short on cash. He wined and dined her, and she fell hook, line, and sinker. The $8,000 Chanel handbag, Mikimoto pearls, and weekly run-around town cash clinched her love. He offered her and her son a beautiful luxury life on the ocean. Beyond her wildest dreams, all came true for Norah.

Once she married him, he changed from the loving, generous husband to the stalking, jealous, old man. She began to despise him. She was depressed, angry, disappointed, and wanted out of the marriage.

He knew it was coming! I never said he was stupid. He knew exactly and pretended she really loved him. His pride, heart and ego were all shot! He tried to remedy this failing marriage. More handbags, shoes, vacations and even a new puppy did not warm her heart. The last straw was drawn. He decided to send Norah and I to an expensive, top-shelf resort for ten days. This was a secret. No one, absolutely no other office personnel, colleagues, clients or friends and family, knew we went to this resort together. Word was Norah was visiting family and I went to Italy. He did not do this out of the goodness of his heart. The Rodster always had a motive. The purpose of this trip was clear. He assigned me to the task of coaxing his wife into staying with him and letting her know how great he is for her! He knew, as the *Office Wife,* she would believe me, and hang in there.

The resort was magnificent. We played tennis, hiked, used the spa, hot tubs, swam and enjoyed every inch of this luxury resort. Every night after dinner, Norah and I would retire to our hacienda and discuss her feelings about the marriage. She freely told the truth and I held that confidence. I have another important note on this little "healthy vacation." They did not allow wine or chocolate on the property—only organic vegan foods. However, I noticed they allow one glass of wine per guest at the Welcoming Ceremony. No brainer for me, who loves her wine. There must be wine on the property. Norah did not care about wine, chocolate yes, but she did not miss having a daily glass of wine. I did, so I took the challenge. After lunch was served, I went back into the cafeteria and met with the chef. I asked him about the wine, more precisely, where is this wine? He laughed and said we have wine on the property, but it is only for the Welcoming Ceremony. I made a deal. I will come by every day and give you $10 for a bottle of white and $10 for a bottle of red. I will not tell a soul! He was shocked that I would even ask. He looked confused, then with a huge smile said, "you have a deal." Another little secret of the *Office Wife!*

So, one evening as we were sitting in the hacienda, I uncorked! Norah was shocked. We sat by the fireside and drank some wine, and she opened her heart and soul. She was troubled, missed home, and tired of his manipulation. I understood and did not coax her into staying. The rest of our vacation we enjoyed all the sports, vegan organic foods, and a bottle of wine every night!

Upon our return, she left the marriage while he was out of town. She called me and said, "I'm gone, and I took everything." She moved fast! Rodney was flying in on a redeye flight at 1:00 a.m. and I knew he was going straight home from the airport. I called him the minute he landed and told him to go to the hotel near the airport. I told him I had the inside of his villa painted and the smell of the paint fumes would not be good for him. I let him know I reserved a beautiful suite in a very posh hotel for the evening. I told him to go there and rest and call me in the morning. To this day, I know he knew she was gone. He did as I said. The next morning, I met him at his house. I did not want him to go in alone and see the empty shell of his home. He acted nonchalant but I could see the tears in his eyes. He blew another marriage.

Colleagues, friends, and family members asked me what happened to Norah. "Silence is golden." I said nothing. I learned the key to respect is to keep the secrets. "They" know what you know, and they respect your confidentiality. *The "Office Wife" keeps everything confidential.* This story holds the basic truth, names and locations that are fabricated to create a tale and honor confidentiality.

It took about two weeks, and he was on the prowl for another nice young lady. He wanted to go onto Match.com. I decided to hire an assistant. I found Betsy, an elderly, retired lady who wanted a little, non-stressful part-time position. Her sole job was to create a profile for him and find him a date on Match.com. That was her entire job!

Betsy and I took the matchmaker job to a whole different level. Knowing how Rodney loved the bizarre and the unusual, we marketed his search by posting custom signs and sending out postcards. They included his picture and his availability and desire to find a mate! It worked. We presented him as wealthy, handsome, and kind. The Rodster was shocked when he found out. He was driving by an intersection and saw his face on the sign! He loved it and gave us each a nice little bonus.

We found his mate! The right and perfect young lady! Sophie Pearson. Once Rodney met her, he was head over heels-again! He felt an instant love/lust. She was in "money heaven." On the first date, he bought her an $8,000 handbag and that gift sealed the deal. It always works! They decided to fly off to Las Vegas and get married in the Little Vegas Wedding Chapel.

What he did not know was that she was a full-blown alcoholic. He never drank. He was very naïve and was blinded by the red flags.

During the day while he was at the office, Sophie was shopping and having cocktails all day. On a particularly gorgeous summer day, the office phone rang and the garbled voice on the other end was proof. It was mid-afternoon and she was drunk as a skunk! She could barely talk and made no sense. I hung up the phone and went to him immediately and said, "Your wife, Sophie, is drunk, and you need to go home." He laughed and did not believe me. I left the office and went to their home. She was sprawled out cold in the master suite, with an empty bottle of vodka and a full coffee cup of Grey Goose near her side. I called him and demanded that he come home—NOW. He did and was shocked when he saw her in an alcoholic blackout. He immediately drove her to the local, prestigious rehab which catered to the rich and famous. After thirty days, he snuck her out without paying the bill. She went right back to her day-drinking and deceit. And he continued to bury his head like an ostrich in the sand.

One day at the office, he complained of pains in his chest. I immediately took him to Emergency and he was quickly admitted. I stayed with him and called Sophie to come to the hospital ASAP.

She said she was on her way. Luckily, I had a list of all his meds. He didn't even know what he was taking. I used to put them on his desk every day with a bottle of water. Sophie arrived three hours later, drunk, and disheveled. She ran to his bedside and hugged and kissed him and asked the nurse if she could sleep with him in the bed that evening. I was disgusted and left.

The following month, my next task was to go visit his estranged daughter, Blaine, at her college. She wanted nothing to do with him or his money. He had been brokenhearted for years over this loss of a child. He asked me to go there, be with her for a long weekend and hopefully prove to her he was not that horrible father she created in her mind. I was successful on that mission! Blaine called him and they talked and laughed for hours on the phone. Their hearts were healed, and they created a beautiful father/daughter relationship. My heart was happy too for them!

Sophie was not a successful relationship. Divorce shortly followed. It was ugly and mean. And was kept very hush-hush. On to the next!

Divorce is contagious in the upper echelon of the successful, ego-centered businessperson whether an entrepreneur, hard-working go-getter, or the trust-fund baby. Wives want more things; husbands want more attention. It's quite a rollercoaster ride! And guess what; you hear all the good, bad, and ugly of this dance, repeatedly. It becomes the "norm."

I am so glad I learned to respect "Silence is golden" early on in my career! What I witnessed a few years later was unbelievable and book worthy. I thought I saw it all with the betrayals of marriage, the unknown secrets of the trades, the lies, the hunger for glory and money, the fulfillment of the ugliest egos, but I did not. There was more to see, more to watch, more to walk away from in disbelief and say nothing.

Ironically, I break no confidence here. This chapter is all about "confidentiality." This story is like a "Twist" ice cream cone. Vanilla is the truth (non-fiction) with a twist of chocolate (fiction). The characters have been embellished to protect their identity. The stories and the tales are very true. This lesson is not just about the rich and famous CEOs of Beverly Hills, Palm Beach, or Palm Springs. This is about the small office downtown in any city of any state or country. The purpose is to teach you the tricks of trade to reach your potential. All support staff, no matter who you work for, can benefit from the guidelines, tips, and tactics. Confidentiality is your golden key.

Years later, I accepted a position with the most humble, brilliant, and easy-going man I ever met. He was top in his field. His ego was love and compassion. He was sweet, naïve and a real "hometown" man. You can almost see him chewing on a hay straw and picking apples. Michael Thomas was a true meat and potatoes man. He fit the Midwest stereotype of loving his pastime of horses, goats, sheep, and chickens. His farm was modest. Simple treasures of life. He always donated generously to the local church. Michael was brilliant. He created patents and prototypes for various local industries. He decided to start his own company in a small town located in the hills of Vermont. I recently relocated and saw a post for an Executive Assistant to the CEO of a local company. The ad was modest, and very professionally written. I immediately applied. Several days later, I received a phone call asking me to interview! Wow! I was so ready.

The interview was conducted in a quaint diner at the foothills. I got there early and waited. I had no clue what he looked like or if he would bring others to this interview. I grabbed a coffee and found a table by the window in the corner and watched as each person walked in. After twenty minutes of watching, a young man in a dark, navy-blue parka walked in. He went directly to the counter and ordered a coffee and a slice of apple pie. Only after getting his order, did he look around to see if I was there. That was him? I waved and he walked over to the table.

What is going through my mind at this minute? What? He did not even offer to buy me a coffee. My past interviews, if not in the office, were at a fabulous restaurant where I was a guest of the interviewer. This was notably a unique experience.

Once I got past that mind thought, I smiled and said hello. He was shy and stressed but sat right down and ate his pie. He really was not equipped to interview. He admitted he didn't even know why he needed an EA, just that his office staff said he did need an assistant. Interesting. Right there, I knew he needed me. He was clueless of how I could possibly undertake the task of creating peace and de-stressing both his business and his personal life. I was confident I would make a difference.

The interview went well. I took the lead and asked him questions. I knew right then and there, he was timid, shy, and needed a strong, organized, and knowledgeable EA. I heard something I never heard on an interview. "I have to ask my wife if I can hire you." WHAT? I just said, "OK, let me meet her."

His wife, Linda, was the opposite. She was bold, strong, distrustful, demeaning, but not the sharpest tool in the shed! She was a challenge. She had nothing to do with his business, but she was the boss! I said what she wanted to hear and softened her hard heart. She even smiled! I was in!

To the public, they were a simple, lovely couple with four, beautiful, young children—ages two through seven. Behind their white picket fence, there were horrific arguments, verbal abuse, and intimidation.

"Opportunity" and "money" knocked on their front door! Accepting a business offer changed their lives forever.

Then, money poured in beyond their wildest dreams. Multi-millions landed in their laps! Knowledge, financial wisdom, and common sense was not part of the package deal! Work no more! Let's play!

Michael and Linda bought multiple million-dollar homes in several other states. They chose one for their permanent residence and enrolled the children in the very best private schools. They generously gifted the homeless and needy with cash, and an open door to their homes. Quite honestly, they squandered not only their fortune but their love for each other and the family unit. Soon, husband and wife became rivals. Each had a deep desire to explore everything and everyone and they did . . . separately. Money was spent on lavish vacations . . . separately. The children were confused and acted in their own way. I witnessed it all. As the *Office Wife*, you watch, you help pick up the pieces, you listen, you hug, you take care of the black and white issues of their lives (bills, maintenance of their homes, housekeepers, landscapers, school functions for the children, groceries, shopping, etc.) But you do not tell a soul. Just know, some wives are threatened by you. They do not want you in their castle, but you really work directly for their husband. Be pleasant with her, and your honor is to your boss. It is not easy to watch their money, relationships and lives unravel into a chaotic mess. It is not unusual. You say nothing to anyone and do your best.

Pain, tears, fears, sadness, and family destruction followed. The divorce was the meanest, cruelest, torturous time of their lives! And it became an incredibly sad time in my life. It saddens you to watch knowing what they had and what they ended up with—a life of "stuff" and pretend, false friends and four hurting children. Their choices. Your job is to honor their challenges and do your best to make this horrible situation easier for the family. You may need to go to court, arrange attorney meetings, wipe tears, hold a hand, and pray with them. You do whatever it takes to ease their pain. How about taking them to get a vasectomy? Oh yes, that happened. His wife "told" him she wanted him to get a vasectomy as SHE did not want more children. He reluctantly agreed. Guess who took him. Me. His wife had yoga! He was like a little boy, scared of the whole procedure. Petrified actually! I waited for him while the procedure was performed. He walked out like he just saw a ghost! His face was drawn and pale, his head was held low. He asked me, "Can you take me for a cheeseburger and fries?" Of course! I helped him into my car and off we went for a burger! All in a day's work of a *"Personal Assistant!"*

The worst pain I witnessed was watching Michael's love of his life stop loving him. His loss was unbearable. Tears and nightmares haunted him for years to follow. He cried on my shoulder daily. I never left his side. I was his friend, his confidant, his Personal Assistant. He was a broken man and brought his wounded heart into his new, single life. Tragic. As a Personal Assistant, your heart breaks as well. You stay strong, dedicated, and confidential. Your compassion for your friend is true and watching him dramatically descend into darkness is heartbreaking. This is the whisper of the *Office Wife*, "Silence is golden."

Treasure Chest Gem: Pearls

Pearls are the ultimate symbol for wisdom. Valued for their calming effects, pearls represent serenity while being able to strengthen valuable relationships and convey a sense of safety. Pearls also symbolize integrity and loyalty.

Pearls are the perfect gemstone for confidentiality. Your integrity and loyalty are on the line every day. It is part of your job to be strong enough to watch the destruction of those you really love and care about. It is their life. Just always remember, it is not your life. If, you cannot divide your emotion from *their* reality to *your* reality, you must leave the position.

You never speak of the inside personal matters to anyone. It is tempting when you are with your colleagues, having a drink after work or gathering at a company event. Know that to build your reputation and move up the ladder to a highly respected and well-compensated *Office Wife*, you must keep secrets.

Secrets that are sacred to your job!
Wear your pearls proudly!

Chapter Three

The Candy Dish

"I don't really remember, but I'm positive that whenever I cried, my mother gave me something to eat. I'm sure that whenever I had a fight with the little girl next door, or it was raining, and I couldn't go out, or I wasn't invited to a birthday party, my mother gave me a piece of candy to make me feel better."

—Jean Nidetch

My next professional venture, I reached out to my infamous gem of a recruiter! In the Personal Assistant/Executive Assistant/Concierge world, you move up the ladder by learning from each engagement and taking it with you to the next level. My personal assistant recruiter loved my most recent experiences working for several demanding, egotistical CEO's and said anyone else would be a piece of cake! I found out that was not entirely true!

I accepted a position as Executive Assistant to the CEO of a well-established construction business. Walter Fischer was a polished man. Built like a drill sergeant, red hair, pale skin with an array of freckles all over his face and hands. Well, that's all you can see of his freckles sticking out of his white starched shirt and tie. A beautiful diamond ring adorned his left hand. His Rolex Submariner glistened money. Walter wore dark suits, white shirts, and no smile. His employees followed the same mandatory office dress code. He was regimented and disciplined from 8 a.m. to 5 p.m. At first glance, you thought he was a character out of the series *Mad Men*. His purpose was to instill fear and respect. And make money, lots of money—the good ole fashioned way—hard work.

I could read him instantly. Anyone that requests to have their pencils sharpened each morning and neatly arranged with the pencil manufacturer logo face-up in the pencil compartment in the top drawer, has issues. Control freak, fanatical, egotistical, good-looking, and if you look deep, deep down, you will find a truly warm-hearted man that was driven for power and money, by working steadfast to be the number 1 in the commercial construction industry.

The Employee Handbook clearly outlined the dress code, work hours, 15-minute breaks, and your lunch hour. All very neatly detailed. Men wore white shirts, a tie and suit. Women wore pant suits or dress suits. No open toe shoes were allowed. Minimal jewelry. Breaks were timed, the one-hour lunch break was closely monitored. Everyone walked in fear. The office air was thick and dreary.

My office was an extension of Walter's office in the "Executive Corner," and it was a very quiet corner! Not one employee dared to venture into that space unless you were part of the Executive Team or were called in for a meeting.

On a side note, within a few short months of my employment, it was revealed that a few select young lady employees got a look—not only at his office—but at all of Walter's freckles!

I would sit at my desk and watch the robots avoid the "executive" area. It was sad, but in a strange way, I knew this had to change. How? No clue. But something had to break this nine-hour day fueled by fear and torture. My ray of sunshine was the Sales Assistant, Gwen, who occupied the desk outside my office. She looked rigid and unhappy. Somehow, I knew she had a fire inside that was being extinguished. I knew we could be great friends! One day she walked into my office and asked me if I saw the wolf on the door. I knew exactly what she was talking about! Secluded in my little office, I spent many hours looking at the wood-grain door. There definitely was a wolf in the wood grain. You could see the ears, the eyes, and the nose. Amazing! I said, yes, and we laughed, and a friendship was born. And to be clear, she was not rigid at all, just unhappy.

I knew the morale was low, and fear permeated the entire workspace. I also knew I had to make a change. A drastic change to wipe out the negative, dark cloud.

I decided to put a bowl of candy on my desk. M&M's always work. That they were all colorful and inviting was the key that opened the door to positive energy. Seriously, when was the last time you refused a piece of candy? Everyone succumbs to the sugar temptation. I knew if I put a bowl of candy on my desk and the word got out, I would make friends. Kind of like the "Kool-Aid" commercial from years ago. Decades before, I worked in a school office. If I put a bowl of candy on my desk—the entire office from students to principals, directors—all grabbed a piece and smiled. Simple. Candy makes people happy.

Little by little they ventured into the "Executive Corner." One-by-one, they would introduce themselves and take a piece of candy and chat for two minutes—still afraid "HE" may come into my office! I saw smiles. Finally, the robots became humanized. Getting to know my colleagues and seeing them smile and share a little piece of themselves was truly amazing. Up to this point, I felt like I was sitting at an airport watching people walk by and you dream up what they are really like, what they eat, what songs they sing, do they dance, live alone or in a relationship, doctors, vets, writers, etc. You just make assumptions and really have no clue. That was what I was doing every day in my office. Not knowing a bit of who they really were. Until I offered candy.

The Candy Dish was inviting. They never hesitated to pop in, grab a candy and chat for a minute even if it was just about the weather, their weekend or their children, husband, wife, or any little tidbit to share. They relaxed, smiled and I began to feel a bond with the staff. I saw the layers of fear peel away like an onion. I knew there was more they wanted to say but were afraid they would lose their jobs.

Months passed and I really got to know a piece about each one of them. They confided in me about how they felt about their job, the hours, the strict dress codes, and the office politics. I found out from these chats that many of them hated their position, but it was a job—clock in at 8 a.m. and clock out at 5 p.m.—watch the clock for that wonderful hour-long freedom lunch.

I attended all the Executive Meetings (CEO, Directors, VP's) and not one word of the support staff was ever made. Sales were dipping and it was a "work harder, stay longer" philosophy. I decided to voice my opinion at one of these meetings. I offered to hold support staff meetings every Wednesday before 8 a.m. I wanted to hear their voices, their issues, their feelings. The executive committee had no clue why I wanted to do this, especially in my own time. In their mind, the support staff does their job. Period. What would be the reason for a meeting with them? What would we discuss? I just let them know I had an intuition and I wanted to move forward. They all saw that I had created not only a working relationship, but there was also a camaraderie among the staff. They said, "go for it." And I did.

I announced to each department that I would like them to come in a half hour early on Wednesday morning and meet in the Conference Room. I knew if I offered food that they would come. Same tactic as the Candy Dish! I announced the meeting and offered bagels and donuts. Done! Food offered; they will come.

The first Wednesday meeting was not well-attended. Two from the accounting department and one from the sales division. We had coffee and bagels. I introduced the purpose of the meeting— to listen to them. I saw the look of confusion on each face. It was like I was the teacher and just announced a pop quiz. These meetings were genuinely created for them. I told them to speak freely about their position—and what would make it better. I promised them I would not share names. I would offer the information gathered from these meetings to the executive committee meetings. I would hold confidence in our group. That was the clincher, confidentiality. They were allowed to bring up things that bothered them.

Each week the attendance increased, and I also took a spin on the meetings' focus. This was not a "bitch gripe" session. It was a session devoted to them.

I focused on them personally and professionally. I listened to their wants and their needs. For example, one department just wanted piped in music because it was so quiet in their area. I brought that up to the executives at their weekly meeting. They hesitated, and I insisted it was important. They did it! Now, that department wasn't leaving at 4:59 p.m. There was no rush to get out of jail! It soothed them and their production went up! They brought that newfound joy to the office each day. It did wonders for morale and sales.

I created a series of twelve sessions—each one had a specific topic, and I always gave them a take-away object for their desk to remind them of the lesson. The series of lessons were based on principles for professional growth and personal development. One session, each participant was given a small mirror. I asked them to reflect on themselves. What do you see? Is that the image you are proud of? Does that image in the mirror scream the YOU that you want to be? If not, what are you willing to do to change that image? Go within and find out who your true self is.? Is that image YOU? If not, go within and examine your true authentic self. The second part of this lesson was to look at your "image" in the company. You work in the accounting department. You interface all day with vendors, banks, etc. YOU represent the company. Your position is vital to the growth of this company. No matter what position you hold: receptionist, accountant, sales, admin. staff—YOU represent the company and are an integral part of the company's success. You are accountable to yourself and your valued position. They listened. They took their mirrors to their desks and reflected. There was a shift from that first lesson to their self-esteem and their productivity.

Word got out in the office atrium and other businesses were asking me to do the same meetings with their support staff. And get paid!

My belief is if you are in an office and all you see are robots—what you are really looking at are just people getting a paycheck and grateful to have a job. What you are not seeing is their truth, their hopes, their wants and needs, their opinions, their ideas, and their smile. All it takes is to break the ice. As the admin. or executive assistant to the CEO, president, or director, you have the power to soothe the tension and relieve their fears. By the way, Gwen followed her dream. She quit her job security and pursued her dream of being a flight attendant. She succeeded and recently retired from her dream job! Dreams do come true!

If you find yourself in an office where all you can think is, "I need to sage this entire building," go buy the candy. Go buy the Candy Dish. Put the dish on your desk and let the magic begin! Show love and compassion and you will be rewarded ten-fold. And so will the employees.

Treasure Chest Gem: Watercolor Gems

Watercolor gems are all different stones, vibrant and shining in their own right. Like a bowl of M&M's, all colorful and different, we each have a contribution and a purpose. Each of our lives both professionally and personally are meant to be seen and heard. Our vibrancy completes the tapestry of life!

The powers of the "Candy Dish" invite compassion, warmth, openness, and truth. I encourage you to read the book, *As A Man Thinketh*, by James Allen.

MARY ANN GAMBLE

Chapter Four

The Gambler

"It's Business. Leave Your Emotions
At The Door."

—Nimisha

We are emotional beings. Women wear their emotions, feelings, and thoughts on their sleeve and all over their face. Men and women may hold the same emotions, but, clearly, women exhibit their feelings—the good, the sad, the bad, and the ugly.

We cannot hold back our tears. The hurt, the anger, the disappointments, and the sadness is overwhelming, and there is no mask to camouflage our feelings. And that is fine! Just NOT in the office. You can cry all the way to the office and all the way from the office. Just do not shed tears at your desk in the office! Take a break—go outside and walk, cry, yell, then put a smile on your face and, as the ole saying goes "fake it till you make it." Walk back to your desk, deep breath and do your job.

If you feel this hellish emotion every day, three times a week, or purely cry on the way to work afraid to face the day and feel anxiety at the end of the day—QUIT. There is always another job manifesting in your future.

I swear, I had the worst job in the world! The position sounded like a perfect fit for me—Executive Assistant to the CEO/Owner of a well-established local company.

It started out nicely. Quite a pleasant office, the staff welcomed me with smiles and "welcome to the family." The CEO was quiet, charming, and intriguing. He was an older "dude" fighting the aging process. Died black hair, tight black jeans and shirts that were trendy and tight. He tried to portray the macho, powerful millionaire. Millionaire—he was. Macho—not so much. I learned that he was a deeply compassionate man with a lack of self-esteem. His name fit him perfectly. Alexander, not Alex . . . Alexander. He and I clicked immediately. He respected my expertise and I respected and acknowledged his passion in his success. He would joke with me, take an interest in my day and was totally warm and friendly and a joy to work along-side. I was also a receptionist. Every morning, he stopped by to say good morning, chit-chat, and genuinely wished me a good day. I always complimented him on his trendy new jeans or shirt. During the day, he rarely left his office. He was working his magic! Before he arrived each day, I would go into his office and polish his glass desk, disinfect his phone, stack his files, and be sure all his Perrier bottles were stocked and label facing forward in his little office fridge. Snacks of almonds, pistachios and macadamia nuts were always replenished and in his silver bowl. Last touch was a quick Lysol spray! I would lock the door, and knew it was fresh and ready for his arrival.

Throughout the day, his office was taboo. He was in the flow of creating new patents, establishing new client relationships, and living his dream. He was the brains, the driving force, and the leader of every department. His select "special" staff were allowed to interrupt him when there was an issue with a customer, accounting issues or any unexpected problem.

This was a driven man. He did not even break for lunch. I would order his lunch, go pick it up and deliver it to him on beautiful dinnerware and silverware. No plastic or paper plates for Alexander. His restaurant choices were 5-star establishments which carried a very high price per meal. Another lunch option. He requested that I make a fresh salad for him every day. Only organic vegetables and a homemade dressing of EVO and lemon. Sometimes, he would have me add some protein, organic of course. I kept all his lunch items in the company's shared refrigerator in the break room. Employees were astonished that I would make his lunch for him every day! They knew not to touch his groceries!

In short, our relationship was steady, respectful, and productive. The employees in the office also respected him and admired his passion. Most were afraid and tried to steer away from his presence. He created a profitable million-dollar business out of his passion for electronics.

My first month, I was welcomed with open arms by all the staff. As the days and weeks flew by, I offered new ideas in systems and processes. They were overjoyed and accepted all I offered. They complimented me on my work, work ethic, and the positive effect I had on all employees. I was offered the opportunity to lead weekly meetings and create a new fresh morale in this office environment.

This "Love Relationship" lasted for quite a few months. Then, trouble in the office marriage! He and I were still holding a respectful relationship. The "special" employees started to resent me. I call them "special," because, let me tell you, they were "especially" mean-spirited, and phony as can be! They were very special.

Within a short time, I felt like I was in the movie *Mean Girls*. I was confused. The irony of it all was this "special" group were the female executives who felt threatened and jealous of my success. In the beginning, I was their "go-to," their new office buddy, their mentor. And then, little sarcastic digs were said to my face. Post-it notes with cutting remarks about an error that they blamed on me. Constant questioning of my work. Is it done yet? Did you file everything? Were you five minutes late from lunch? On and on they went, stronger each day. I never, in all my career, felt like I was back in high school! They did everything in their power to slam remarks at me, question my punctuality, hand out ridiculous tasks, and smiled while they were doing so. I always smiled back. Keep cool. Lower the shield of hurt and anxiety. Smile. The "mean girls" were just waiting for me to break. They would smirk at me after a demeaning comment. They prayed for tears. I watched them go out of their way to criticize me in anything they could, even if it was a lie. Every emotion was streaming in my mind and heart. I held strong, took a deep breath, relaxed my shoulders and posture . . . and smiled. My lunch hour was filled with tears and anxiety. I hated it when the hour ended. I watched the clock. At 4:45 p.m., I would inhale and exhale relief.

In the evenings at home, I was angry and depressed. I ate comfort food and had no energy for exercise. I gained twenty lbs. of stress fat.

The CEO was clueless. I knew his allegiance to his executives was strong. I could not and would not confide in him or anyone in the office. This lasted one year. The worst year of my career! One that I still think of, and cringe. I had to practice what I preached: "Check your emotions at the door."

The final straw was drawn when I emailed "Cinderella's stepsisters," as we are instructed to do, to request time off for an upcoming doctor's appointment. In the *Employee Handbook,* it stated we needed to give three to five days' notice. My appointment was five days out. They declined my request. In an email, they told me I needed to give them three weeks' notice. You do not deny a cancer patient their follow-up doctor's visit. I had completed radiation, and cancer no longer lived in my body. But, like any cancer patient, you must go for routine ultrasounds, blood work and doctor visits. Mine are every six months. I let them know my doctor requested this appointment after reviewing my recent lab results. They knew exactly why I had an appointment. Thus, they are called the "Mean Girls."

Once I received the denial for my doctor's appointment, I felt so angry. I wanted to yell and scream "HOW DARE YOU?" I calmed myself. I did not cry. I smiled. I kept smiling till I was laughing out loud! I laughed till tears ran down my face. They just lost their game plan which was to find joy every day trying to break me down to tears and fears. Hell no!

I decided to do something I would NEVER advise anyone to do!

The next week, I cleaned out my desk a little each day. I cleaned up everything that was personal on my computer. I kept smiling and pretending all was well. I held my composure and projected a happy, positive employee. They despised me more each day. I chose the following Tuesday to make my break! It was a cold, wintry day. Snow was piling up in the employee parking lot. Salt trucks were out, and a winter storm watch was in effect. I left the office at 5:00 p.m. and said good night to everyone, my usual closing. "Good night, drive safely and see you tomorrow!"

The next day most businesses were closed. Schools and banks were closed. The storm dumped six inches of snow. The streets were icy and treacherous. But our office was open! I had NO intention of going into the office—whether it was a winter storm or a sunny, summer day. I was a no-show. There was no way in hell, I would go to work at that office ever again!

I received numerous texts from the "mean girls" asking me to show up to work now! They made it clear that this was not a day off. I did not reply. The texts continued non-stop. Texts asking me if I was running late, if I thought it was a "snow" day, and that it would be in my best interest to show up or call them ASAP. Not one text asking if I was OK, or if everything was alright in my life. I could have been stuck in a snowbank and all they cared about was that I was not stationed at my post!

I believe it was around 10 a.m. when they finally realized they would never see my face again. That was my plan, almost. I emailed the owner around 1 p.m. and told him quite frankly, "Please be sure your witches never tell a cancer patient or any employee they cannot meet their appointment, especially when the Employee Handbook guidelines have been met." He was shocked and apologized. I smiled. No tears.

Over the years, I witnessed plenty of support staff cry in the bathroom or at their desk. I vowed never to be one of them. I prided myself on being able to hold my emotions at work. This was a real trial that I was facing eight hours a day, five days a week.

When I look back at that year, there were so many times I wanted to cry. So many times, I wanted to tell someone in the office how horribly I was being treated. So many times, I wanted to yell back and slam the door and walk out. My emotions in the office turned to depression at night. My life was in chaos, and as much as I loved the work, my health was more important. Remember to not allow your health to be in jeopardy no matter what it takes.

Treasure Chest Gem:
The Black Onyx Crystal

Black onyx crystals can be used for grounding, protection, and self-control, and as a shield against negative energy. Black onyx has a calming quality, which can be beneficial in working with challenging emotions such as grief and anxiety.

Hold your emotions intact. Do not allow anyone, no matter what their position is, to enjoy the outcome of their meanness in watching you cry. Hold your head high. Do not cry. Do not throw a temper tantrum. Do not even try to tell them how you are feeling, because my dear, they don't care.

Leave that job anyway you want! Quit, get fired, just be done with it.

A take-away that I later used in my classes with support staff to ease your emotions is to place an object on your desk that you love. I placed a heart-shaped shell on my desk. In times when tears were ready to flow, I would hold the shell and force a smile. Fake it till you make it! The trinket will ease your mind and help you get through that moment.

You will not believe how wonderful your next job will be! You have learned a lesson and will carry it with you for the rest of your life. Once you release yourself from hell, heaven is around the corner! It is sweet!

**Remember the lyrics from Kenny Rogers'
"The Gambler"**

"You've got to know when to hold 'em
Know when to fold 'em
Know when to walk away
And know when to run"

MARY ANN GAMBLE

Chapter Five

Anything Is Possible

"If you have a strong belief, then anything is possible."

—Hermann J. Steinherr

What do you do when your boss asks you to do something that is totally beyond your capability or experience? Something you have neither heard of, nor a clue how to go about this project. I will tell you, there is always a way, and you *will* find a way. First, you rely on your intuition, you stop and think. What is your first gut thought? What is the first thing that comes to your mind?

Let's play a game. Your boss comes in and says to you, "Please, by the end of week, arrange a phone conference with the President of Hallmark." You reply, "Hallmark Cards?" He says, "Yes, that's the one." You ask if he knows the president or has any contact info from the past. He laughs and annoyingly lets you know he doesn't even know who it is. There you go! Now what? What does your gut tell you? This is impossible, or I don't know how, but I know why. Go with the latter and you will accomplish the impossible! First, with confidence, you begin to research. You lower the shield of anxiety and google like crazy! Now you will learn that *anything is possible!* Stretch yourself and know you got this—

somehow, someway. Once you tackle a task that you never thought, in your wildest dreams, you would be able to pull off flawlessly, your self-esteem will rise to the top and so will you!

This task was a challenge, but I held my confidence and figured it out. Finding the phone number of the Hallmark CEO was neither a challenge nor was that my goal. My strategy was to get to know his Executive Assistant. She/he would be my key in this pursuit. I knew that she/he and I would need to create a relationship before an appointment was confirmed. So, I researched and found the office number. Eleanor Hart was his assistant. She answered and politely let me know he—Mr. James—was not available. I thanked her, and said I would call another time. And, I did. The next day, Eleanor answered the phone but she seemed agitated. She quite firmly replied, "No, he is not available." That was my prompt to make conversation. I said to her, "Don't you just love trying to keep track of their calendar? It's impossible! Especially when they leave the office and make appointments and don't tell you. That is the killer of all!" She laughed and said, "You know it!" We chatted for a while and I said I would try another time! The next day, I called. Eleanor answered, "Hi Mary Ann, how are you?" Now . . . we are friends. I told her I was swamped that day, but my boss keeps insisting that I keep trying. I laughed and said, "Like this is all I have to do today!" She laughed and said, "I hear ya sister!" She asked what was the purpose of the call? I told her, "Quite frankly, I don't know." We laughed and agreed that we sometimes struggle with being in the dark . . . and just proceed with the task. Eleanor then offered a date and time! BAM! I did it! The appointment was made—success!! I put the phone down, went directly to my boss and let him know the date and time I had reserved for his appointment with Mr. James. He was shocked! Now he had to make up a purpose for his call. Mission accomplished, appointment scheduled by the end of week! Eleanor and I remained friends for years!

How? How do you do the impossible? It starts with believing in yourself. My past challenges as I was a school secretary for fifteen years were limited. The challenge was to be promoted to the higher education levels in the school district as Secretary to the Principal. As my daughters moved up in the educational school system, so did I! Watching your own kids be called down to the Principal's Office due to bad behavior, etc., was the biggest challenge! Other than that, the secretarial skills were basic. Each day, behavior issues were the highlight. Maybe a kid threw mashed potatoes in the cafeteria and hurled the meat loaf to another student? Sometimes students were caught climbing out the window, smoking pot in the parking lot, a teacher forgot their class key, and sometimes the principal forgot a meeting. Nothing dramatic. Nothing earth shattering. That goes to prove—experience is not a prerequisite for doing the impossible!

Being alone in a new state, the loss of my lifetime partner and empty bank accounts is totally devastating and depressing. I had moments of severe loneliness, depression, lack of self-esteem, guilt and suicidal thoughts. I started my day by reading and journaling. I found Louise Hay's *You Can Heal Your Life* to be my lifesaver! I realized through this daily practice that I had 2 choices—stay still and suffer or get up and move forward. Louise Hay's book was the foundation of my motivation! I had no hesitation in applying for a legal assistant position of which I was not even closely qualified! It turned out that this position was a "captive position" to David James Steiner. A 43-year-old spoiled brat. I found out quickly how demanding someone who had the world handed to them on a GOLD platter reacts to the "Help." I was the common folk, the "Help."

Flexibility was key in this new job. Day One was eye-opening, astonishing, and revealed exactly how strange this job would be. There were no other employees in this office suite. Just me. Dressed in a gorgeous Ann Taylor, sky blue suit and bone-colored high heels, I sat in my new empty office. There were three file cabinets. Each held a maximum of ten files. The walls were stark white and there was not a picture on the walls. His "pretend" executive office had pictures of yachts, gala events he hosted, his wild party scenes, movie stars, well-known sports figures, and, quite strangely, pictures of him as a little boy on family vacation in Europe. Beautiful mahogany furniture and Italian leather chairs filled this suite. I stared at my office's blank walls and waited for "The Master" to call me and tell me his "demands" for the day. That call happened everyday around 2 p.m., which was his wake-up time. The usual requests to be taken care of immediately after his daily call were to order sushi to be delivered to his home, dry cleaning delivery, prescriptions delivered *immediately*, and an array of nonsense requests. The houseman would call me to ask for assistance in preparing the evening meals and managing the renovation of his latest residential property. In all, he owned six homes. At 4:00 p.m., his bodyguard would arrive at the office with wine, cheese, and crackers for me. He would wait in the office with me until 5:00 p.m. At 5:00 p.m., the houseman would call me, and I was beckoned to David's home office. There I would wait surrounded by the obnoxious luxury of his home. I sat at the lavish pewter bar and awaited my name to be called into his office. Grey

Goose Vodka was flowing, shrimp cocktail, lobster tails, oysters, and an array of cheeses. All little perks of the job! I would find his bodyguard alongside "The Master." Gun on the desk. Very little eye contact and few words. Just brief, vague instructions for the next day. Sometimes, I would wait as little as an hour, other times it could be up to 3 hours. None of this made sense, but it was intriguing, and the compensation was generous. During your wait, you can drink the best of all liquors, Grey Goose Vodka, Far Niente Chardonnay, order lobster tails or whatever your heart desires. There were no limits. His staff included his personal photographer, driver, private executive housekeeper, houseman, private residential landscaper, and others. We all ordered food, drank well, and all agreed—this was strange but in a strange way—very fun!

I'm sure you get the picture that this assistant position was like no other! Office hours were 9 a.m. – 5 p.m., however, his demands were 24/7. He never came into the office. The Robb Report, NY Times, Newsweek, People, and other magazines and books were delivered to the office and my job was to read the articles and chapters he was interested in and write a synopsis for him by end of day. I attended numerous charities and promotional marketing events to view various products in which he may want to invest capital. I hired, fired, and managed personal photographers, landscapers, private housekeepers, handyman positions, pool services, and pest control. No office work, no memos, no emails, no calendar . . . just on call for his needs! From 9 a.m. to 5 p.m., I read the articles and wrote a synopsis on each, answered numerous telemarketing calls, and waited for my next task—whether it was finding a particular CD he was interested in, pick up dry cleaning or kids from school, or whatever he wanted at any time of the day!

He hosted lavish events at his home, country club, or yacht. The events varied from black-tie celebrity attendance, sports figures playing a round of golf at his country club, or the party people on his yacht. Along with that, he always requested an escort. I was responsible for picking the right one! There were notebooks. Each one is titled for each category of event. Each escort had a profile, which included their likes and dislikes for their welcome gifts, their flight preferences, cocktail choice, favorite candy and—believe it or not—Victoria Secret's wish list. I looked at their profile, photograph, and matched the right escort for the event.

And that, my friend, was my first job in my new home location! Soon, it all became routine, and I understood my role, I received a phone call at 10:00 p.m. that evening. I was alarmed and thought something was wrong. Did I do something wrong? Was the wrong dry cleaning delivered?? Oh no, did he run out of his prescriptions?

At the time of the call, I was finishing dinner with a friend at a local restaurant enjoying a fine meal and delicious wine. "Sorry, I know it's late but . . . (The word "but" totally negates anything said before it.) I need my special diet tea from one of my houses and I need it by midnight." Remember, the call came in at 10:00 p.m. And . . . a little tidbit about his whereabouts—he was on an island! Not far from the mainland but on an island! I knew this was his game, to test me and challenge my abilities. I am not going to lose this match! Game on!

I called the houseman at his primary residence and asked if the" special diet tea" was there. He found it! Luckily, it was the right house, as he owned several on the mainland.

Next, I called car service and had them pick up the tea immediately and bring it to the marina. I started calling the marina—repeatedly. Remember, it's now 10:30 p.m. and no one is there! I called consistently for fifteen minutes. Finally, a gentleman answered in a rough, rushed voice "What?" I was so elated that there was a voice at the other end of the phone! I asked who he was and if he could help me. I told him exactly what I needed. I asked, begged, him to take the tea from the driver, which would be there in 10 minutes, grab a boat and deliver to the island. He said he was there working on a boat for a customer. "Not my boat," he said. All I cared about was I had a live voice on the other end of the line.

I explained again that a car would be dropping off a red box of "special diet tea" that needed to go to the island by midnight. He replied, "Lady, I can't do that!" Can't? Oh, yes you can! I offered him $2,000. He changed his tune. Now, he can! And he did! The tea arrived at the island resort by midnight! My boss called me at 12:15 a.m. and said, "it arrived." I replied, "I know. Have a good night. Talk tomorrow." I was in shock! I did it! I smiled and slept like a baby! **Anything is Possible**!

This job showed me how to pull all the tricks out of my hat! To know, no matter what the request, I can make it happen. I didn't always know HOW, but I always knew WHY. Because I can! And so can you. Expect the unexpected. Be prepared with confidence in yourself.

Treasure Chest Gem: Brass

Brass is an alloy of copper and zinc, of historical and enduring importance because of its hardness and workability.

Know you can. Even if what you believe sounds impossible—now you can make it possible. Change your mindset and strategize. Visualize the end-result of YOUR challenge. It really is a mind-blowing experience to accomplish some task or assignment that sounds like the craziest request, the most absurd—and you wonder—I know the "why" I must do this, but I don't know the "how." Trust me. You will know the "how."

You possess the strength and ability to adapt, perform and be successful. It's all a game. Go in knowing you will win! I promise you, you will.

Chapter Six

BEFORE #MeToo There Was Me

"Women who accuse men, particularly powerful men, of harassment are often confronted with the reality of the men's sense that they are more important than women, as a group."

—Anita Hill, *Speaking Truth to Power*

Did you know that approximately 54% of women experience some type of harassment at their job? You may think it won't happen to you. My friends, it may happen tomorrow! Or, it may have already happened, and you are in denial, fear, or confused! There are many forms of harassment. You need to clearly identify what is happening. Sometimes, we put it off and ignore what is going on to save our jobs! You don't want to get fired, right? Who would believe you? So, you shut up and put up. It is the scariest, demeaning, fear-filled and lonely experience of your life. And it is one of the biggest challenges of your mental and physical health.

At the time, I was very content with my job of three years, and not searching to change. Once again, my favorite recruiter gave me a call and said, "I have the right job for you!" I thought I had the right job. Well, this one paid 25k more than my current job. No brainer! I accepted the interview appointment.

This opportunity was for a high-level Executive/Personal Assistant to the CEO/Founder of a large (200+ employees) manufacturing institution. The founder was a mild-mannered man, the opposite of my past experiences. Soft-spoken, brilliant, honest and a man of integrity. I admired him and the business he and his father created in their garage in 1969.

The interview went smoothly. He was impressed with my resume. I was hired that day!

When I gave my notice to my current boss, he agreed that I deserved the financial upgrade, and we remained in touch. He was happy for me and congratulated me! Class act! He and his wife took me to dinner to celebrate! A year later, when I was going through a divorce, he and his wife were right there to support me and celebrate my decision to stop the insanity of that marriage. To date, this kind couple and I remain friends.

This new position was grand! However, I was the lowest on the totem pole in seniority. I was immediately hired for the top administrative job and my peers shunned me in the beginning. It took time, but they trusted me, liked me, and soon treated me like part of the family!

Lloyd Levine was a quiet, soft-spoken, gentle man with a compassionate heart. He was fairly low maintenance (compared to my past employers). My job was quite easy and not demanding at all. His daily routine was very rigid. He woke up at 5:00 a.m. every day and stayed at home and worked from there until I called him at 10:30 a.m. This call was to remind him he had one-half hour to finish his work and get ready to go to meet his personal trainer for his morning swim. Then, I would call his personal trainer and let him know Lloyd had been warned. 10:45 a.m., I would call again and remind him and ask him to call me when he gets in his car. He obeyed! Once I received his call, I would call his trainer and let him know Lloyd was on his way! That may seem high maintenance, it is not. It is part of the job! At 11:45 a.m., Lloyd's housekeeper brought his lunch to the office. I then readied this noontime meal for his arrival. Room temperature water poured in a Baccarat goblet, placemat, silverware, white cloth napkin that was starched and folded in half, and all food emptied from their containers and artistically placed on a Raynaud platter. When he arrived at the office, he always acknowledged me with a big smile and went directly into his office suite. I always had to remind him to stop and eat his lunch before the afternoon appointments.

Lloyd would get lost in his work. Ten minutes before each appointment, I would go into his office and remind him! He always acknowledged me and smiled. Five minutes before, I would tell him to follow me, and I would escort him to his appointment. I stayed for the appointment and took notes. He never carried a pad or a pen. He walked to each appointment with his calendar— the old-fashioned, loose-leaf daily calendar. He also carried a pencil to jot notes. Most of the time, he was so intrigued with the discussion he did not take any notes. That's why I was there! Lloyd carried the burden of not only leadership of every department but the writings of all articles, manuals, publicity, and speaking engagements. He was calm and carried on. He was a fabulous leader, husband, father, and friend to all.

I respected him and loved working for him. I also had numerous other basic secretarial duties of filing, making appointments, travel arrangements, etc. It was pleasant! I was in a beautiful corner office in "Executive Row." I loved this job, I did it well and it was gratifying. I was always grateful.

Business was booming. Employees were happy. We had moved into a beautiful new building with an in-house drycleaner, cafeteria with different ethnic stations, and the most beautiful views of the sea. What could be better? I loved all my colleagues, and we were all happy campers!

Being privy to the executive discussions and decisions, I knew Lloyd was overwhelmed and needed some assistance in day-to-day leadership of the organization. The Board agreed. They decided to begin the search to hire a president. Lloyd was relieved. Now, he could spend more time with family and travel the Asian countries and African safaris. Sounded like a GREAT idea! The newly appointed president would oversee the directors of each department and report all business back to Lloyd.

Human resources handled the process of hiring the new president. You must know this was a highly successful global entity, so confidentiality and discreet processes were of prime importance. Even I was not privy to the background checks, hiring process, etc. After months of searching and interviewing, the choice was made. The board made a formal announcement that the new president would be joining our group soon! We were all excited and anticipated the welcoming of a new leader to assist our beloved Lloyd.

We learned the new president was moving from Mill Valley in Marin County, California, and bringing his family to our East Coast. The announcements of our newly elected president hit the local news and radio stations! We all awaited his grand arrival.

A week before his arrival, two gentlemen came into my office and asked where Dwight Richard's office was located. Ahh, Dwight Richards that was the name of our new president! I let them know his start date was not for another two weeks and he was home in California with his wife and children. They started to ask me questions that intuitively seemed strange to me. They asked me where we found his resume. They asked me if we had received references from his previous positions. They asked me if we had performed a background check and if we had the results. They asked me if we interviewed him in our office or via a phone call. They asked if anyone in our office had an in-person meeting with him and his wife. I had no answers for them. They looked puzzled, and I reassured them that this was a very confidential hire, and no information was released other than a new president was hired.

I offered to escort them to the HR department where their questions could most likely be answered more completely. I never heard a word from HR who the gentlemen were or why they were visiting our company. Later, I found out they were the FBI. Interesting.

Two weeks past, and the new president, Mr. Dwight Richards, arrived! Lloyd was visiting a family in another country at this time, so I was selected to show him his private office, and a tour of the corporate headquarters. I scheduled meetings for him to meet with each department head and key employees. I was also asked to find an executive assistant for him from the staff we had already employed. I chose several assistants, and Mr. Richards did not want any of them. He also asked me to NOT call him Mr. Richards, but "please call me Dwight" and he gave me a little shoulder hug. He asked if I could take on dual duty and work for him as well. I would agree to do so if the CEO approved. I knew I could handle the workload of both Dwight and Lloyd. It is true that in some corporations, the higher your position, the less work you really must do. Departments report to you with their statistics and info for the CEO and president. Organizing meetings, events, and calendars is your main priority. Seemed simple enough for me!

This new President, Dwight, was extremely likeable. A huge smile and a fantastic sense of humor. In a very short time, he was the star quarterback for our team. All the employees loved him and respected him. He had several one-on-one meetings with each director and gained their loyalty. He also asked me to organize one-on-one meetings with every employee, all 250! He preferred the meetings to be scheduled during lunch or after hours. I was reluctant to schedule after-hour meetings, so I lagged back on that assignment. A few of the female employees came to me and said he wanted to meet them after work for a drink for an informal "get to know you" meeting. None of them were willing to meet after work hours. I respected that and scheduled lunch meetings *in* the office.

Within a two-month period, some alarming and strange things started to take place. I was confused when several calls were being sent to my office phone asking for Mr. Dwight Richards. Unbeknownst to me, he had all his calls transferred to my phone. The calls were regarding his personal unpaid bills: cell phone, gas and electricity, mortgage on his California home that was up for sale, his insurances, car payment and even his children's school tuition. I also learned from these calls that he took out a huge loan from his brother who called daily for payment. Dwight had no intention of paying it back. He also had the same name as his dad and forged documents with his dad's social security number and refinanced his dad's mortgage and scammed the money. How did I find this out? One day, his dad called the office, and, of course, the call was transferred to me. He sounded very weak, he was crying and clearly in shock. They were on the verge of losing their home and Dwight was responsible. How do you answer that? I told him I was sorry, and I would do whatever I could to remedy this situation for him. I went in and confronted Dwight. He denied it and said his father had dementia. End of story.

Dwight's wife and children rarely visited. He was scheduled on several occasions to visit them, and I later found out he had no intention of heading back to California to visit his family, Oh no, the American Express card showed flights for two from the East Coast to Hawaii. Not a family visit.

We had a huge company-wide party, including all our vendors, our clients, the local news, and the town supervisor to celebrate Dwight's arrival! Surprisingly, his wife and children attended this gala event. It broke my heart to see the love and admiration his family expressed for their "hero," their beloved husband and father. Somehow, I knew, deep down, this man was not who he said he was, and I strongly believe his family had no clue.

Many times, I scheduled flights and made hotel arrangements for meetings with potential clients, and I would receive a call that he did not show up for his confirmed appointment. Time after time this occurred. I would call his cell, and he never answered, nor did he call the office. Days later, he would call and claim he either had food poisoning from a meal he had the night before travel, or he woke up in the morning of travel and had the flu and could not make it to the airport. He declared he was home sick and not well enough to let us know. I, of course, had to make the calls to the clients, apologize, and tell them Dwight was very sick and cover for him. It became routine. I was beyond suspicious. In the beginning, I thought it was my imagination and I was thinking nonsense. I soon realized my intuition was spot-on and I was not delusional. This man was a liar.

What could I say? What could I do? This company and the Founder (Lloyd) loved this man! I just kept quiet and observed.

Monday mornings became another fiasco. I would arrive at the office around 7:45 a.m. and prep both Dwight's and Lloyd's office for the day. I always wanted to be sure their calendars were updated. The cleaning staff wiped down their teak desks. Pens, pencils, notepads, water in the fridge and morning snacks—all in order. Dwight's office became a Monday morning nightmare. The first time was a shock. After that, it became the norm. What did I see? I will tell you. There was always a hint of cocaine on the desk. There, a white smudge of lines had been left, a rolled-up dollar bill, and sometimes marijuana cigarettes that were once lit and smoked and now just thrown on the desk. Oh, the lovely surprise of ladies' undergarments in the drawers. I even found ONE high-heeled red shoe left behind! Small airplane bottles of rum, whiskey and bourbon were scattered throughout the room. It was a disgusting mess that greeted me on Monday morning! I threw it all in a large garbage bag and dumped it in the outside dumpster. I questioned Dwight and he just laughed and said "clean it up" with a broad smile and a wink. Made me sick to my stomach. He told me if I told anyone they would not believe me, and I would lose my job. If I left the mess, he would be sure I would suffer the consequences. Then the big smile and wink. If I was a person who threw up easily, it would have burst out of me. Instead, I just felt queasy and numb. I went back to my desk and pretended all was well.

That's the killer. That's what messes with your mind and your body. That is what happened to me.

One morning, Lloyd asked me to take Dwight to find an apartment in the local area close to the office. Dwight was late almost every day. He said he was staying with a friend who lived about 40 minutes from the office. Right. Lloyd's thinking was that an apartment closer to the office would be beneficial as a shorter commute for Dwight as well as a place for Dwight's wife and children to come and visit. They were in the process of selling their California home and needed a place to stay while visiting. Seemed like a fabulous idea to Lloyd. Dwight would be close to the office and his family could come and stay with him during the kids' school breaks until they permanently moved to the East Coast.

That added another element to the hell I was experiencing daily with Dwight. This brought the behavior to another level. An Alfred Hitchcock nightmare. This occurred fifteen years ago, and to this date, even though it is years later, the memories are fresh and the sick feeling I carried back then is fresh and nauseating.

Doing as I was asked by Lloyd, I researched apartments and made appointments. I scheduled all appointments during the workday. I let Dwight know what my task was, and he thought it was so kind of Lloyd! He was overjoyed that "we" would find his apartment.

So, all the appointments were made, and we were off to visit the local apartment complexes. At that time, I had a very small two-seater car. I chose to drive my car and escort him. Dwight flipped the switch on the car ride. He was very flirty and kept telling me how grateful he was for my assistance. I smiled and replied, "part of the job." He never took his eyes off me. He started with the compliments . . . how pretty and sexy I looked, how he couldn't understand why I was single, etc. He told me that every day he looked forward to seeing me in my suit and high heels. He told me my legs were amazing. I said nothing. Just drove. The flirtations continued. I was starting to feel extremely uncomfortable. I am very claustrophobic and get sweaty in tight places and my anxiety skyrockets. This happened! I said nothing. Then, he slid his hand on my thigh and rubbed my thigh up my skirt. And he laughed and said, "it's OK." I shivered and knew I should remain calm. I could not. I was in shock and fear. I told him to STOP, and he laughed. He laughed and laughed and said, "I didn't mean to scare you!" Too late.

We arrived at the apartment complex, and he acted like nothing happened. We got out and went in to meet the manager. The location was close to the office, reasonably priced and wonderful amenities. I decided right then and there this was the ONLY apartment we would visit. I wanted this fiasco to end and get back to the office. We met with the property manager and Dwight filled out the application. We went through some model apartments. At the end of the tour, the property manager said she would review the application and background check and get back to us ASAP.

On the ride back to the office, I kept the conversation light, and the radio turned up loud.

He became sullen and moody. He seemed fearful or maybe it was defeat.

Later that afternoon, I received a phone call from the property manager. Dwight was declined due to his credit score and background check. His credit was not up to par! What? This is the president of a large corporation. Bad credit? Trigger! Something is up with this dude. When I told him the results, he laughed! He was not alarmed at all. No questions were asked. He accepted it and laughed it off. But I could tell he was shaken and now had to face Lloyd with some truth of who he was, or will he?

Lloyd called and asked me how the apartment hunting went that day. I told him Dwight was declined. He was furious and questioned why and how that could possibly have happened. He thought it was a poor decision and blamed it on the fact that he was new to the area and they had no past landlord referrals. It was a misunderstanding, in Lloyd's view, because Dwight was recently hired and not fully established in the area. I told him, no—that was not it. The property manager was aware of his position and his resume glowed with outstanding accomplishments. His credit is bad. His background check conflicted with Dwight's story. Lloyd was shocked. And so, the nightmare continues.

Dwight's advances and flirtatious episodes towards me increased . . . daily. I was not the only target. As I mentioned, he was attractive with a contagious laugh! And he appeared bright and knowledgeable in business matters. The staff loved him and thought he was doing a great job for the company. Some questioned his family situation and others commented they saw him out at bars and restaurants with other ladies. That was swept under the rug! A few of the female administrative assistants whispered to me that he had asked them out for drinks after work to get to know them. His original plan that I refused to execute. The admins. all rejected his offers as they felt it was a bit creepy. I knew it was. Little did they know what I experienced.

I started getting little messages in my emails. "You look hot today," "Your legs are amazing, want to wrap them around me?" and other sexual pop-up notes. I printed and kept copies of all. He continued to send them throughout the day, every day.

One day, I was sitting at my desk, and he came up behind me while I was typing and slid his hands down the front of my shirt. I jumped and he covered my mouth. He walked away and laughed! I was frozen with fear and shock. When there was no one else in the executive "corner," he targeted me. He loved scaring me. He knew the fear he instilled in me, and he loved it.

Each morning, Dwight strolled in late to work. He had to walk by my desk to get to his office. So many mornings, I noticed he had a white substance around his nose. Cocaine? Yes. He was wired and foaming at the mouth. In a disgusted voice, I told him to go wipe his face.

Finally, I found an apartment complex that would accept his application. It was a month-to-month rental in the low-income part of town. I hired a cleaning staff to clean it once a week, just in case his family arrived, I wanted it to be presentable for them. One day, I received a call from the cleaning lady. She was crying and said the place was so disgusting she could not clean it. She asked me to come there. He was traveling, so it was safe for me to go there. I arrived and there were garbage bags full of dirty clothes—some male, some female. Empty bottles of brandy and bourbon and drug paraphernalia. Glasses everywhere. Throw-up on the carpet. Bed with no sheets just a dirty mattress. It was filthy. I told her to leave, lock the door and I will handle it. We left. I called Merry Maids, and they went in and cleaned. I could tell no one about this. Confidentiality. *"Office Wife Secret."*

My birthday is in February, right around Valentine's Day. On my birthday, I was in my office working, and Dwight wished me a very Happy Birthday and I looked up and nodded. A few hours later, I was filing in Lloyd's office, and Lloyd was at a doctor's appointment. Dwight came in and cornered me, pushed me against the wall, and planted a huge kiss on my mouth and said, "That's your first present." He walked away and laughed. I cried tears of fear, shame, and anger.

"Don't you dare say a thing," was his new line. He would whisper it, write it, or mouth it with no sound. I was drained and weak. After a while, no tears. I was frozen in fear and felt paralyzed by such abuse.

The instant messages became non-stop; "come and sit on my lap," or "drinks tonight?" Each time one popped on my screen; I became nauseous. He always followed with "Our little secret."

What do I do? Tell the Founder? Tell the Board? Will they believe me? Will I get fired? I needed this job. It paid so well. I lived in fear. Even a whisper of this secret that I held daily would destroy my job. I prayed. I prayed for courage and strength. I prayed for the lives of my family that were being threatened. I prayed for help! By the grace of my Higher Power, I decided to move out of my frozen state and act! I saved every little note. I journaled every little comment and gesture. I kept a daily log of all the harassment. I kept a note of everything! All the missed flights, pictures of his Monday morning office, everything I could find, I documented.

During this time, I noticed he was receiving FedEx envelopes marked Personal and Confidential. He hired outside vendors for various projects for the company. I opened the mail. As a Personal Executive Assistant—"Silence is Golden." You can open the mail, but if it is a **Personal and Confidential** matter, you know NOT to discuss it. They were checks for large amounts (5k, 10k, 15k) all made out to him, personally. Kickbacks from his good ole boys! Corporate theft by the president of this world-renowned corporation! I took pictures and kept a record of those checks as well. I was dumbfounded that the CFO was not aware. Looking at his corporate credit card—it was black and white! Expensive dinners and bottles of wine, offshore betting, outrageous hotel bills, flower deliveries to Hawaii, jewelry store purchases, even a Hermes scarf! In his desk, he even had receipts for lap dances! What was going on? I recorded it all.

This went on from February 12 to July. In late July, he showed up at my apartment. It was 10 p.m., and my girlfriend had been over for dinner. She just left and I failed to lock the door. I was doing the dishes and suddenly, he was standing there! Drunk and strung out on cocaine. He pulled me into my bedroom and threw me on the bed and started to take off his pants. He was so drunk; he couldn't even do that. He was falling and hanging onto my leg. He started to bite me on my legs and arms and torso. It was hell. I kicked him off and ran out of the bedroom and told him to leave or I would call the police. He said if I dared, he knew where my daughter and granddaughter lived and would kill them. Oh shit. Now what. Who can I call?

Visits to the house continued—late at night. I *always* locked my door and never answered, and he never entered again. However, he would leave me notes: "Open the door next time," "I know you are in there," "I will kill you." "If you say anything, I will kill your daughter and granddaughter; I know where they live." I kept all the notes.

In August, I had a stroke. My anxiety level was out of control and my BP off the charts. The stress of the sexual harassment, threats to my life, physical attacks, and the knowledge of the president's corporate fraud, lies, drug use, infidelity and secrets paved the way to my sudden stroke. I was in the hospital for three days then sent home for 10 days of bed rest. That was the final straw!

During my healing time, Lloyd called me at home and said he and his wife were praying for me, and hoping I was healing well. I was speechless at first. I was filled with compassion for Lloyd, who trusted this man and had no clue what a monster he really was. Then, I regained my determination to honor myself.

For months, I knew what a scoundrel this man was. I was the victim that suffered his sexual harassment and abuse. I had a stroke—time for me to talk. It was a blessing that my stroke did not leave me with any permanent physical damage. Oh, I could walk and talk, and remember all the harassment. Mentally and emotionally, I was scarred for life. I was going to use my powers and strength to reveal this man's true identity. I was done living in fear. No matter if I lost my job, or my reputation, it didn't matter. I needed to honor my Sacred Space that he violated.

I asked Lloyd to meet me on Saturday morning for coffee and be sure to come with the head of Human Resources. I created *my* agenda for that meeting. He was receptive and continued to let me know how sorry he was for my illness. He had no clue about the details of my presentation.

We met at a local Marriott. I wanted to meet on neutral grounds. Hugs and smiles from both Lloyd and Brad, the HR Director. Compassion and willingness to offer me comfort and security in my position at the company.

First, I presented all the financial facts and the corporate theft and lies. They were alarming to both Lloyd and Brad. I showed evidence of kickbacks and credit card charges and multiple receipts. They were astonished! I looked at Brad and asked how could the CFO of this large institution not see the charges on Dwight's corporate AMEX? He put his head down and was silent.

I revealed his father's calls to the office, crying and revealing that Lloyd had stolen his identity and refinanced his mortgage and never made the monthly payments. His father and mother were at the point of losing their home. How could they have missed that? I asked them, "Didn't you think it was a bit strange to have the FBI arrive at our office a week after hiring him?" They believed the story he told them. He told Lloyd and Brad that his former college roommate (of years ago) was selling drugs and caught, and they just wanted info from him. Lie!

I showed them the pics of his office after a wild weekend of partying there. Pictures revealed the true character of this man. They tried not to look at the pictures, but took in every detail of the clothing on the desk and floors, cocaine lines, razors, empty bottles of brandy, and even the red high heels! I told them about his disgusting apartment and the fact that cleaning companies were disgusted and most would not even take the job of cleaning this filth. The look of shock on their faces was priceless.

With tears in his eyes, Lloyd thanked me for telling the truth and making him aware of a bizarre situation he knew nothing about. And, of course, saving the company that was built by him and his dad through hard work and faith. Dwight cost the company hundreds of thousands of dollars! Their cash flow was suffering, and it was all making sense to him. They thought the meeting was over.

They were so wrong! I moved onto Part 2 of *My* agenda.

I let them know that I asked HR to be at this meeting for a reason beyond the financial mess Dwight created. I wanted to discuss *my* sexual harassment. Back then, this was not talked about. Women just shut up and suffered. The fear of telling someone and not be taken seriously kept the secret hidden. You would lose your job. And, for some, that was the money that put food on the table and shoes for their kids. And, the disgrace you would suffer by others who would now look down on you in disbelief. There was no "Me Too" movement. This type of abuse was swept under the corporate rug. I made them aware the stroke I suffered was not just bad luck and I had pictures, notes, and bruises to confirm my harassment. Dwight caused the anxiety and fear that led me to a stroke. It was the "President's" fault. He sexually, verbally, emotionally, and physically abused me.

I proved my point. I put all my cards on the table for their view—every note, every recorded threat on my cell phone. Everything I collected. I showed them the notes in his writing how he threatened my life, and my daughter's and granddaughter's life. Notes that said "Where are you? I will kill you if you don't answer your door next time." Scratched on a torn piece of paper he wrote notes in his drunken/ drugged state. I showed them pics of the multiple bites on my body. I explained how he pulled me into my bedroom and threw me on the bed, and started biting me and tearing off my clothes. I told them he did not sexually penetrate me as he was so drunk and drugged he could only bite me. I told them how the fear stiffened my body and how his heavy hand over my mouth drew me into a state of shock. I couldn't breathe or scream. He was done, I kicked and finally was able to push him away, he grumbled something and left. He didn't shut the door. He left it wide open. I ran and slammed and locked the door. I sat there for hours and cried. I did not call anyone. I just cried. I wanted them to hear every detail of what happened to me! I journaled every day, and yes, I let them read my daily logs of abuse. I wanted them to read every day's entry for the detailed past five months of hell that I lived. It was painful to reminisce. Writing this chapter is somewhat therapeutic as those thoughts of that time period have been buried for many years.

They were shocked, saddened, and speechless. Their faces showed fear of this unknown new president. They looked at each other. Neither one of them could look me in the eyes.

With their heads down, they reassured me that on Monday morning they would have security escort Dwight out of the office. He will be fired on the spot. They advised me to visit my family for a couple of weeks because Dwight would most likely be full of rage and may go looking for me. I told them, "Hell no! He knows where my family lives. Let me think about this and *I* will let you know where I will be staying." I was in control. Rightfully so. Amen.

The meeting ended abruptly after my Part 2 agenda. I felt the heavy weight of five months of anxiety and fear lift from my body. My body was weak, but my mind was relieved. Refreshed. I went directly home.

Once home and alone, there was a still small voice telling me "Mary Ann, honor yourself. You have been harassed. This is NOT OK." I listened to my intuition this time. I really didn't know what to do. I never shared any of this horror story with any friend or family member. I had to reach out to someone. Someone smart, savvy, and proactive. Bam! I knew exactly who to turn to. My next-door neighbor, George. He was always there for me with advice, a joke to cheer me up, a helping hand, and a financial loan when needed. And he was smart, very smart, and shrewd.

I went to his condo, which was 3 steps away! I told him my entire rendition of hell and all that transpired over the months from my birthday in February to the end of July. I explained to him the reasons I had a stroke. I wanted him to know the steps that led to my disaster. He listened with compassion. George looked at me, smiled and said, "You are not alone." That was a gift in itself. He then said "Get the phone book and let's find an attorney. Darling, we will take care of this!" You see, back then we only had the "yellow pages"—no Google!

We searched for employment lawyers. There was one name I was familiar with, as I had done some temporary work when I first relocated. He was an outstanding attorney at the firm, personable, knowledgeable, and never lost a case! I called him and left a voice message.

Three days later he returned my call, and we scheduled an appointment at his office. I offered him all the company documents I copied, the nasty disgusting sexual notes from this "President," all the pictures—including the graphic bites on my body, notes of death threats to me and my family, the AMEX business card charges, the evidence in pictures illustrating the cocaine use in his office and an entire calendar of multiple misses flights. I informed him of the FBI coming to the office. He knew I had a case. This was serious.

In the meantime, I decided on where I would "hide-out." I picked a 5-Star, well-known, East Coast, megabucks resort. I once worked there as a catering assistant to the members' golf leagues and knew the security staff and the fabulous food and accommodation. And I loved the golf course! I would be safe and in luxury. I chose the Jr. Suite—at a price tag of $1500/night. Today the rate is $3,500/night. It is a gorgeous suite overlooking the waterway. Amazing accommodations and amenities! That was my plan and George was coming with me!

I called Lloyd and told him my decision and that ALL charges would be to the company. Food, stay, golf, purchases, EVERYTHING for two weeks. He humbly agreed. Off I went to "THE" Resort with George. Every day he would leave and go to work on his yacht, and I would be by the hotel pool, shopping in the luxurious boutiques and planning which restaurant we would dine in. He would come back to the hotel, and we would have the best culinary delights ever imagined. Sounds wonderful, right? The pain and fear I suffered stayed with me EVERY moment. Money and luxury cannot heal. It's an inside job! I was constantly looking over my shoulder. Hearing Dwight's voice in my sleep and seeing his hands on my body. Knowing I was still employed and needed to report back in two weeks always shadowed the bright glitter of every day.

I returned to the office and all the memories poured back into my mind, my soul, my body. I could smell the odors of Dwight. His cologne permeated throughout the office. In my mind, I could see the trashed cocaine office. It was as if I was reliving a nightmare. I looked into his office through the glass wall and became nauseous with memories. My phone smelled like his cologne. The reminders were torture. Each employee that I had contact with shyly smirked and some sort of smile was forced. They all knew I was a victim. Many of them also suffered a mild "Dwight harassment," but again, too fearful to say anything as their job was on the line.

Lloyd was already in his office. That was totally unusual, as he never came in before noon. Remember, I had to call him every morning! Something was up! Sure enough, he called me to his office.

With a saddened look, he told me that because of the financial doings of Dwight the company must cut back staff. And, because I had the least seniority and the highest salary, they decided to let me go. I knew that was coming! I replied, "That's just fine with me." And I meant it. I was nauseated. And I knew, and let Lloyd know—that I knew too much for them to keep me there as an employee. This was not hush-hush. The staff knew what happened. I smiled and said, "That is fine, see you in court."

I hired an attorney and went through the process. The process was grueling. Lie detector tests, multiple questions asked several million ways, and multiple repetitions of what happened, where it happened, when it happened, how it happened, and reviewing all my documentation.

We all decided mediation was the way to go. That worked for me. Seemed simpler than being in court. It was NOT easy. Sitting in the room, facing Lloyd, his wife, the HR staff, other managers, and company staff was hell. They acted in disbelief that anything like this happened. I was making it all up! This was hard for me to swallow because I knew them, and I liked them all! I snapped out of it and realized honoring myself was of premier importance.

We had two days of mediation. I felt this was going nowhere. Same questions of my honesty. Hell, I took several lie detector tests and they all proved in my favor! I was NOT lying, and they knew it.

My attorney was great, knowledgeable, professional, etc. The opposing attorney tried to portray me as a liar, seductress, and scorned. This did not bother me, as I knew (and prayed) the truth would win!

Day 3 and I decided enough is enough! I told the mediator and the attorneys that I wanted to meet with Lloyd alone. The mediator said that was not allowed. I had endured enough abuse and was taking control of my situation. I silently said a prayer, took a deep breath and mustered up the courage to say, "Don't tell me what is allowed. I'm paying you."

Lloyd and I met in another conference room alone. He was humble and shy. He was polite and kindly asked what did I want? He was willing to offer me $5,000. I laughed and told him to add zeros to that number. I told him that is not even close to what I believe is due to me. I told him a minimum of $500,000. He laughed and said, no. That is too much money. What would you do with that money? I was in shock, he actually asked me what I would do with all that money! I remember that moment like it was yesterday! I let him know it was none of his business. He stressed the cash flow of the company was not good, since the president finagled hundreds of thousands. I told him that was NOT my problem. I wanted a percentage up front (enough to pay my attorney and a chunk of money for me). The rest he could pay monthly until my settlement was met. That settled his "cash flow problem."

He agreed and we settled on a generous amount. The attorneys and mediator were shocked! My attorney congratulated me for my good work!

And it was done. I spoke up and honored myself! I went through all the emotions, the stroke, the pain, and I stuck with my gut feeling and pursued justice.

Years later, I have not healed from this harassment. You are never completely healed. You remember with pain. You remember every second of it. You release it and move on. The pain is as strong today as it was then. I wrote this chapter of my book today and I feel fear and helplessness with each sentence. I know this story has a lesson. And I know writing it is like a deep healing meditation for me.

TREASURE CHEST GEM:
The Golden Nugget

A golden nugget is a chunk of valuable information. It could be a life lesson, a marketing tip, a quick fix, an "aha" moment, or it can change your thoughts which changes your actions.

If you are uncomfortable with the actions of another employee, employer, colleague, or the mailman—action must be taken. My advice is to keep a journal from the very first encounter. A diary of any events that made you uncomfortable from words to actions is your ammunition. Anything in writing via email, text. Keep every piece. Save all voicemail messages. **Do not wait!** Collect and report to human resources. Evidence is key. If you do not think HR will believe you, hire an attorney. There are employment attorneys that will support you and will not charge a fee unless you receive compensation.

Again, as I say throughout this book—Honor Yourself!

As an executive/personal/administrative assistant you are privy to behind the scenes of the business. If you notice foul play on the part of ANY employee, keep notes. No matter if it is the CEO, Vice-President or any level of employment. There are a lot of uncovered secret wrongdoings in some businesses at every level. The founder/CEO/owner is in the dark with most of these happenings. You may see something and think it is your job to take the "ostrich" method and hide your head in the sand. It is not. Again, collect your data— keep copies of kickbacks, wrongdoings, anything you know is underhanded and hurting the owner's company. And report! It is your job to do so.

If you are not proactive, it will bite you in the butt! The mental and physical anguish you will experience is the basis for hypertension, cancer, TIA strokes, heart attacks and immune system shutdowns. I have had them all! You must release the dark into the light and honor yourself. Do not let anyone or anything disrupt your peace, your power, your dignity, or your divine destination. And so, it is.

Chapter Seven

Your Invisible Fence

"You best teach others about healthy
boundaries by enforcing yours"

—Bryant McGill

Build Your Boundaries!

As an "Assistant," whether it is personal, executive, administrative or concierge, we tend to "aim to please." Right? We do what we are told to do, accomplish what is expected of us each day, smile, speak politely, say "yes" even when we want to say, "Hell No." We nurture egos, buy the supplies, make the coffee, organize the files, keep all calendars, make all appointments, make nice to all we encounter all day long—no matter what. As assistants, we are an integral part of service and hospitality.

Well, my friends, all of that is not who *you* are, and you need to *STOP and SET BOUNDARIES* right in the very beginning of your employment. You deserve the same loyalty and respect! You will recognize this type of bullying right from the get-go! Knowing your boundaries and strategy to implement them daily is part of your wellness! It goes hand in hand with *honoring yourself*. It's not a white picket fence, nor is it an iron fence gate—it's an *invisible fence*. You create your fence and no admittance is allowed to anyone or anything that trespasses on your wellness, your morals, your integrity, your values—your life.

I learned this very critical lesson through trial and error. I loved every high-end, demanding, professional, executive assistant position I was offered. I excelled at each and every one with zeal, passion, and pure gratitude for each engagement. I found myself going above and beyond the "call of duty." It was a fun, fast and furious ride with the elite and rich! Then, I realized working 24/7 was self-sabotaging. Yes, the money was great. The perks were amazing! I was selling my soul with no boundaries or respect for my time, my life. That's when chaos shows up.

In 2005, I was hired as an executive assistant to an outrageous character who held his ego high and mighty. This office was recently relocated, and his assistant quit in the process. There were boxes and files all over the entire office. Not only did I have to study him, his work, his product, and what my position would entail—I had to create a new office space.

I was hired the day of my interview—right on the spot! My 9 a.m. interview kicked off my first day of work. This office recently (the day before I was hired) relocated. The previous executive assistant quit and was angry. Needless to say, the files were a mess! I went through piles of files, not knowing what anything really was, smiled politely at my new boss, and just put my nose to the grindstone. After all, this was Day 1—I needed to impress him!

At 6:40 p.m., I was exhausted. My new ego-driven boss was still in the office talking on the phone, drinking his coffee, and showing no sign of ending the day. I was beat, exhausted and had a major headache. You know the feeling? Drained. I let him know I was closing shop for the day and would be back at 9:00 a.m. the following morning.

He laughed and said to me "I guess you don't have what it takes to do this job!" That hit me like a ton of bricks across my already aching head.

He was standing over me, as I looked up at him from my desk chair. My face went beat red and I knew I had to do something now! I stood up and asked him to sit down for a minute, *please*. This physical act gave me the strength to look down at him . . . like he had just done to me. I quietly and firmly said, "Don't ever talk down to me like that again. That comment was inappropriate, and I will never allow that in my employment here or anywhere. You tried to intimidate me, but that doesn't fly with me." He looked shocked (I loved it!) and he said, "Yes, Mary Ann, I was wrong." I thanked him, smiled, and told him I will see you tomorrow! I was shaking in my boots! Where did that come from? I never in my wildest dreams thought I would have the gumption to stand up for myself to any man—anywhere! He created a trait within himself to antagonize anyone in order to feel superior. He loved to intimidate office staff, clients, competitors, and family members. I knew his reputation before I started working for him. I knew he would be challenging, but I also knew it was a high-paying, interesting position that I could fulfill. Done! My first "Boundary" was set!

Oh, that didn't stop him. Even though I erected my "Invisible Fence," he jumped at every opportunity he could during the first year to intimidate me, until I showed him that I was not playing the game. Never play that game. Build your "invisible fence" and be sure to add on the "zapper." Let them feel the shock of your boundaries. Put the imaginary collar on everyone and zap them when they try to invade your sacred space! Your boundaries will become known and you will be treated with respect and honor. And that's what I'm talking about!

I worked tediously and completely managed the office and his life. I hired and fired staff. I handled all the accounting and worked closely with our CPA. I managed his calendar, his daily appointments, all the various business entities, bookkeeping, office personnel, as well as his personal appointments, his children's expenses, his household finances, buying of presents for family, friends, and mistresses, and even hiring and firing household personnel and girlfriends! He traveled extensively to promote his business and his many ghost-written books. I managed all travel arrangements and venues, power point presentations, client relations and marketing. I was on overload and decided to hire an assistant to help me with data entry, answer phones, file, and later, between his divorces and marriages— she handled all his dating sites! When I took a short vacation to visit family, he fired her. Upon my return, I hired her back! I became the core of his business and his personal life. I respected that position and held it all in confidentiality for several years. I knew more about his personal and business life than anyone knew. His flaws, his character defects, his loyalty, and his dishonesty.

The letdown of all my allegiance to him personally and his business was summed up in a moment. I was visiting my mother, who was ill with cancer in my hometown. She was dying and my time with her was limited. My flight was to arrive back in time to be at work at 9:00 a.m. on a Tuesday morning. Well, that morning of my flight, she had an early doctor's appointment. It was not my duty to take her. My dad already planned on taking her to the oncologist. It was my love for my cancer-stricken mother to be there for this appointment. I would not miss this appointment while I was visiting. My heart spoke clearly.

I changed my flight to arrive back to the office at 1:00 p.m. on Tuesday. I called "the intimidator" and let him know. His response was so egotistical! Why was I shocked? He smugly replied in a deep, monotone, ". . . if you are not here in this office by 9:00 a.m., don't come in ever again." Damn! He without knowing it—just fired me! I let him know exactly right away, "You just fired me!" Be on the lookout for unemployment forms! He didn't believe me.

He fought it . . . hard and strong. He denied all circumstances that led up to my filing for unemployment. We had a hearing scheduled at 1:00 p.m. Of course, he missed the appointment. I was not there to remind him! I won. Unemployment started immediately. Did the triumph make me happy? No. It did not. If you are a dedicated assistant and do your best, it is not a triumph. It is more a matter of integrity. Honoring yourself. That's a tough lesson, but once you learn it you are changed for life!

Out of the professional world, and now into your personal world. How many times do we say yes when we mean no. Many of us don't even think about how we let ourselves fall into the catering of others' needs. Why? Because it is hard to say no. When you are a giver and have a nurturing personality, you are constantly "on demand." So many of us, men and women of all ages, are not even aware of how they are dishonoring themselves.

Our children, our spouses, our ex-spouses, our parents, our friends, and our colleagues somehow rank higher than your own wants and needs. Doing something you do not want to do destroys your inner peace and self-worth. For years, I said yes to everyone and everything. Little by little, my confidence was non-existent. When I was alone and divorced, I said yes to every outing and invitation as I didn't want to be alone. I was wandering around for inclusion, friendship, and love. Learning to say no, and being alone is the premier present you can give yourself.

Set your boundaries each day. Plan your quiet time and hold it precious to your heart. Take a walk—anywhere alone! Sit and journal. Get in nature. Get grounded—take off your shoes and feel the earth below your feet. Grounding soothes your mind and body. And if you are asked to go to an event, dinner, babysit, or even something extremely exciting and your intuition says "no"—listen and say, "No, thank you." You will feel refreshed and free. Set your boundaries now with whomever or whatever you are overextending your time and energy. Your health is more than diet and exercise, vitamins and supplements, self-help books and affirmations. Your energy is to be recognized and guarded. Find your space each day to be with yourself for yourself. And choose wisely. Keep your boundaries!

TREASURE CHEST GEM:
The Yellow Diamond

The yellow diamond is rare and more expensive than the clear diamond. It sparkles the same but is a different gem. Be the yellow diamond. Sparkle unlike the others.

Always remember this little story. It is the prerequisite course to becoming exactly who you know you are. Exactly what you know, you can accomplish. Exactly the success you will manifest! When you first start a new position, you are not always aware of what boundaries need to be set. Each position is different. You will quickly realize the agreements you will need to create to keep your sanity and honor. Watch, listen, and do not make any assumptions. You will intuitively know what is necessary to fulfill the commitments to this position and yourself.

Know who you are.

Do not let yourself and your boundaries down.

Never let your guard down.

Stand strong, work hard, and reap the well-deserved financial compensation while holding your <u>peace</u>.

MARY ANN GAMBLE

Chapter Eight

When It Sounds Too Good to Be True,
It Probably Is!

"If it is too good to be true . . .
it is probably a fraud"

—Ron Weber

Throughout this book, one of my main mantras is *Honor Yourself,* meaning holding boundaries and knowing your worth. I believe that mantra should flow through your mind every day and in every situation. Work is no different. Yes, you are getting paid to do your best, and we all go overboard. I always asked why assistants push themselves harder than most employees. Do we do this out of the need for recognition or money? Do we need to prove our worth? There are multiple reasons, and all are valid. WE all do it.

I achieved every executive assistant, personal assistant, virtual assistant's dream. I was in demand! I was receiving calls from the executive assistant placement agency every week about various opportunities, even though I was employed. I refused all interviews as I was quite happy in my current job.

I had an interesting job as an executive/ personal assistant to a workaholic full of drama and energy! It was quite a challenge, but really fun! Just imagine Steve Catrell aka "Michael Scott" from the TV Series *The Office*! That was my boss. He surrounded himself with quirky characters. One colleague, Joey Franco, was a great match for craziness in both his professional and private life. His solid gold Cartier necklace and bracelet was always in full view through the opened collared shirt. Sparkly diamond rings on each hand and a smothering scent of cologne. Louis Vuitton wallet and man-purse displayed his worth to the world! He was a successful entrepreneur. Whatever he touched turned into gold, 24k gold. He started from ground zero and created a magnificent following. He was a talker, eloquent and polished, with an incredible sense of humor. He could schmooze the top CEOs around the world. He was intelligent, and you knew it from the beginning. He loved to speak to large audiences, and he grew ten feet tall with each accolade. He portrayed himself as a man of truth, honesty, compassion, and luxury. All were attracted to him, his work, his books, his style, and his wealth. He was always working on new ideas and was a master con artist. He visited our office on a regular basis and he and I were respectfully friendly.

One day he visited while my boss was traveling and told me about this new world-wide master plan. I listened and told him it was remarkable, and I truly loved the idea. It sounded exciting and challenging—my passions fulfilled! Joey asked if I would join his team and bring this idea to fruition with him. I replied, "not now." He pursued me relentlessly. A fast-talking, smooth operator in full force! Joey didn't take no for an answer when he wanted to hear a yes. Today, he remains a prominent figure to millions. Therefore, I will respectfully keep his identity anonymous.

After a few months of constant pursual by Joey and promises of doubling my salary along with a healthy bonus, I decided to jump on board! My current job was great, but in this line of work, if an opportunity of greater compensation and room for growth is offered—take it! My title was Director of Operations, with a promise of a hefty salary and bonus program. "When it sounds too good to be true, it probably is."

I joined the team at the beginning of the creation of this mega million-dollar venture. I was part of the brainstorming, the business plan, statistics, and the next step to the day of the launch! It was an incredible experience, and I was extremely grateful for the opportunity. I worked with brilliant men, women, well-known authors, and speakers. Each facet of this program was exhilarating, and motivational. The main ingredient to this whole project was ONE MAN. A renowned author and leader. He was always in the public eye. He was a respected prominent figure in the industry. His name alone would attract thousands. My involvement was intense as well as a dream come true!

After the launch, the project was swiftly underway! Joey Franco partnered with this 'infamous gentleman" to attract fans all over the world. He already had a mass of fans. This new project will create even more.

We started from scratch in an old warehouse. My office space was limited with a desk, conference table, chairs, and a printer. We all met around the conference table with pots of coffee, pens, notepads, and ideas. Ideas were bouncing off the walls!

Day 1 was successful. An e-blast to a current database of Joey's followers announcing the launch of this newly created program was sent. The driving force for response was an offer to be recognized on a video by sending in your name and an affirmation that changed your world. Of course, everyone sent in their name and affirmation with the dream of being seen on a worldwide broadcast video. That was the initial step to attract the masses. And, it did. Next phase was to rent a studio and Joey would make a 2-minute video saying each of their names and their affirmation. The video encouraged others to send in their reply so they, too, could be "seen" on the video. The next push was the sign-up for the program of entrepreneurship, leadership, and financial wealth. The response from followers was overwhelming. A week was not enough to accommodate all the responses. So, the second session was already in the planning stages!

The back end administrative work that needed to be done to get to this launch was crucial. And that was my assignment! I spent long hours and long days to develop the systems and processes to make this the most outstanding program offered. My passion was very much a part of this creation! I spent hours in the office, weekend meetings and ran errands as needed. It was thrilling to be a part of the planning stages and watch the brainwaves of knowledge flow in high energy. Brilliant group of people creating a world-class program. I witnessed strategy, and knowledge above and beyond! What a gift!

To accommodate the registration, we needed to rent an entire venue. That alone was a major undertaking. So, I left my in-office administrative tasks and ventured out to find the right and perfect venue! Once the contracts were established, I was on-site daily even before the event. I worked with the chefs to create the week-long menu. I tasted all entrees, snacks, beverages. I checked the executive suites to be sure they were stocked with all the speakers' choices. I checked each hotel room for cleanliness. I checked the public bathrooms available to be sure there was enough of all paper products and soaps. I checked every nook and cranny of this venue. I had the wallpaper in the main ballroom washed down, wallpaper corner tears repaired, fresh coat of paint on the doorframes, and the carpet scrubbed. All looked good! It was a go! Joey's motto was ". . . don't tell me about the labor pains, just show me the baby." So, all the conference arrangements were my responsibility with no questions asked!

Back to the office to set up the registration process, hire temporary assistants, arrange cocktail parties, book-signing events, and multiple other perks for the registrants. It was my job to organize a flawless registration. 500+ people were attending! One venue could not accommodate the number of sleeping rooms needed. I found an additional hotel to house the overflow of guests. Each registrant also was offered a packet. Another task of mine was to write study guides for the speaker's books that were being offered. Each participant received 3 autographed books and 3 study guides for each. That packet also contained various marketing materials for their use for their own entrepreneurship. The autographed books was another day of planning. A conference room needed to be reserved, temps hired to help unpack and repack each book. The author would be handed a book, sign it, and the temp would pack it back in the box. I hired temps to put one of each book in the goody packet for each participant. It was a long process, but it was part of the promise made to lure the registration.

All the speakers needed assistance in creating flyers, study guides, and their individual meet and greet sessions. I was their assistant. I made sure all materials were printed and ready. I arranged to have their beverage of choice on the lectern for their presentation. I arranged meeting rooms for their "meet and greet" sessions.

I created a staff "when and where" calendar detailing where each staff member needed to be and the time. I told them this was their "bible" for the next 3 days! I managed the processing of name tags The tags were alphabetically placed and ready. Registration, guest packets, hotel venues, transportation, meals, and all the amenities were in place. Speakers had their materials. Signage was up and we were ready to open the doors!

By the way, my salary did NOT increase. The promise changed. The "double salary" would be reflected in one healthy check at the end of the sessions.

The event begins! I worked at the registration booth in the morning and roamed the venue all day to be sure all was going smoothly and on schedule. I did periodic checks of the restrooms to be sure they were stocked! I examined each food item before it went to the buffet. It was a long week of smiling, doing and being. I clocked in 18-hour days and probably walked millions of steps! I crashed each night in my hotel room only to do it all over again the next day. It was a spectacular success! Lots of money was made for the key players. I was promised $25-35k at the end of a huge undertaking as a bonus plus my "double salary." That was peanuts compared to the profit they made. However, it was huge to me! I was honored and so grateful.

Finally, it was the last day of the conference. It was about 3:30 p.m. and I went outside for a breath of fresh air. I watched everyone enjoying their dream! They paid thousands of dollars to attend this convention and were thrilled at the realization that their future can be changed dramatically! They were energetic and full of hope. I was mentally and physically exhausted. I hit my limit. I never worked so hard in my entire career. At that moment, I promised myself never to work this hard to make someone else rich, especially someone who was not grateful for you, your dedication, and your integrity to work as many hours as needed to fulfill their dream.

My relief was in knowing all the long hours behind the scenes, the months of planning was over. And now for my bonus—my payoff for the sore muscles, drained body, good works, excellent management, flawless organization, and mental exhaustion.

And then . . .

Bam! Reality! There is NO bonus. Just your hourly salary which was nothing more than I had working at the other company. The "bonus" money was allocated to the projected expenses for the next session. The verbal promise of "after the next session" pierced my ears. I had not signed a contract. I trusted their word. The lesson I learned in Don Miguel Ruiz' book "The Four Agreements" clearly states "Be Impeccable With Your Word." Apparently, they never read this book! My fault. My lesson. Bogus bucks next session? I quit! I walked out, held my head high, and stared Joey right in the eyes and said, "I was disrespected and lied to by you. Your words are meaningless, and your promises are fraud. Your program is for the foolish." That's all I could do. My legs were shaky, my hands sweaty and I was hurt, right to the core. You move on. You learn the lesson and you move on to the next event. Quickly and with ease, I did!

The *"Office Wife"* secret. On the outside, everyone thought I was making a great salary working for these highly successful, well-liked by the masses, individuals. No one knew I was overworked and underpaid. I smiled and kept on going, while my spirit was telling me to stop.

I'm telling you now to STOP. No matter who your "Joey" is—friend or family or someone you just admire. Don't allow it because the bitterness you hold inside your being destroys your health.

To this day, I still don't believe how I was taken advantage of by very successful men, who did not care one bit about me.

I chalk it up to experience, but I never will say it was OK. I feel disrespected and will never allow that again in my professional life. My message to you: Always do your best and demand compensation. Be sure to have a contract if you are working on a project with a monetary bonus that is above and beyond your daily scope of work. We started each meeting with a prayer for the team, the program, and all members involved. Just know that even the most Christian, generous, famous, well-adored leaders, and entrepreneurs could fail you. Why? Because they don't care.

Treasure Chest Gem: The Opal

The Protective stone. Do your job to your best ability. PROTECT YOURSELF!

Do not overwork your body and mind to the point of illness. My story is not unusual in this high-profile arena.

I felt scammed. And I was disappointed. Once, twice . . . but never again!

Honor yourself and know your worth. Be clear. When promises are made to you, be sure to have a legal contract drawn up and fully executed.

Chapter Nine

Know All There Is To Know

"To acquire knowledge, one must study;
but to acquire wisdom, one must observe."

—Marilyn vos Savant

We are in a constant study mode! We study people. We listen to how they talk; we watch how they walk. We love "people watching." People, places, things, animals, you name it, we watch. Social media is a prime example, especially Facebook. Many just observe. They do not partake. They just scope it all out. Little stalkers!

We grew up studying for exams, studying mathematical equations, the history of our land, the scientific breakdown of molecules, our language's grammar, and everything under the sun we needed to graduate. Before we bought our first car with our own hard-earned dollars, we studied the sticker values, the Kelly Blue Book, features, colors, miles per gallon, etc. Now we were buying our first house. Let's check out the neighborhood, the taxes, the crime rate, the amenities, the appliances, right down to the electrical wiring. Now let's go on vacation! We study travel, Airbnb units, "things to do," TripAdvisor, and we gather advice and knowledge from friends and family who have traveled to our vacation destination.

We research everything all the time! According to Google, research is "the systematic investigation into and study of materials and sources in order to establish facts and reach new conclusions."

What's my point?

I'm here to tell you most of us miss the MOST important subject to study—*YOUR BOSS!*

Your new boss is your main study—day in and day out—from day #1 on the job.

You will achieve your master's degree in this subject. Doors will open and opportunities will be abundant, and prosperity will flow!

We all walk into a job with as much knowledge about the company as we can cram into our head. Before the interview, we went on the company website and read all we could about their product, the "About Us," the software used, their marketing techniques, the location, testimonials, salary ranges. Our first impression is the interview, and we want to come across as knowledgeable about the company and its product. It works! We get the job!

Day 1, we walk in, greet our boss, colleagues and sit at our new home away from home desk. We "notice" what he/she wears, smells like, speaking manners and all that meets the eye. Day 2, we are in the onboarding process of learning our new 8-5 day's tasks. Our days fly by and we become a successful attribute to this family. Not replaceable, but valuable.

I will teach you how to be the most profitable asset to your boss. And it all will come naturally. You will STUDY the subject and your value will skyrocket.

Listen. Listen to how he reacts to certain conversations. What restaurant did he just rave about and why? Hear how the tone of his voice changes when speaking to different folks. When he hangs up the phone, does he comment negatively or positively? Listen to how his voice fluctuates when he speaks. Listen to how he talks to his family.

Listen to how he talks to prospective clients. How does he treat his employees? Is he a "coach" or is he condescending? Listen to his laugh. Is it hearty? Is it real? Can you tell the real laugh from the fake laugh? Listen to his mumbles. Listen if he slams the drawers to his desk after a phone call. Listen. Be alert. Listen

Watch. Study his mood when he walks in the office. Watch if his head is hanging low. Watch if his shoulders are back and he is walking straight in the office ready to tackle the day. Was it a good morning at home? Is there a spring in his step or slouched posture? Look at his face. Is there a frown and lines on his forehead? Or are his facial muscles relaxed and a slight smile when you greet him. Watch.

Memorize. Memorize his health issues. How often does he go to the doctor? What type of doctors does he go to and why? Know his medical status—no matter what age. Jot down on a pad or on your phone all his medications and the dosage of each Ask him. Tell him you need to know as his assistant. It's valuable knowledge. I have taken my boss to emergency with heart issues and luckily, I had a complete list of his meds that he could not remember. Know.

Buddy Up. Get to know his close friends and colleagues. Speak to them on the phone in a friendly manner. Take interest in them. They are the whipped cream on top of this man's life. The cherry on top is his FAMILY. His siblings, parents, kids, grandkids, wife, ex-wives, cousins, aunts, and uncles. They must trust you, like you, respect you and admire how devoted you are to their family.

It really comes naturally if you are truly devoted to assisting this person in his/her life. If you do not respect this person—quit. The stress and anxiety will rear its ugly head and your health will suffer. Leave, say good-bye, and move on. Life is too short to hate your job, and there are so many wonderful opportunities out there waiting just for you. Always hold your trust in The Law of Attraction.

Know everything you can about the life of your boss. EVERYTHING! What do they eat? What is their favorite cologne/perfume? What color of clothing do they wear most of the time? What mood are they in today? What makes them laugh? What makes them upset? What is their passion? Do they have a hobby? Introvert or Extravert? Risk taker? Know their scent, their tone of voice and then study some more. Earn your master's degree in mastering your subject.

This "study of the subject" is an *Office Wife* secret. I cannot stress the importance of this tactic. Knowledge is everything. Once you know your boss inside out, you hold your power and your confidence in doing exactly everything in harmony with your "assistant" position. It's not something listed as a qualification or in the job description. It is not necessary to hold the position. It is beyond the qualifications. It is wisdom. It is knowing. It is the golden key. You need to know what he/she needs before they know they need it!

Treasure Chest Gem: Lapis Lazuli

Lapis lazuli is regarded as the Wisdom Stone. At every stage of our life, we acquire wisdom. When we are children, we learn and become wise to the consequences of disobeying parents, breaking school rules, and disrespecting friends and family. As teenagers, we challenge what we learned in our younger years, and, again, the consequences of rebelling teach us to know what we can and cannot do. As adults, trial and error plays an important role in absorbing the wisdom to trust your intuition in relationships, finance, and our jobs. We learn, and we move forward with the wisdom of the lapis lazuli gem.

Use your intuition to know. Use your eyes and ears to study. Use your mind to absorb. Your wisdom unlocks the door to freedom, peace, power, and unlimited adventures. This knowledge is the bridge from an "Executive Administrative Assistant" to the "Office Wife."

MARY ANN GAMBLE

Chapter Ten

Let's Go Virtual

"Productivity is never an accident. It is always the result of a commitment to excellence, intelligent planning, and focused effort."

—Paul J. Meyer

Rise & shine! Wash your face, brush your teeth, and put the coffee on. Scrambled eggs, hot buttery biscuit and sweet, creamy steaming coffee—breakfast is served! Now, the journey to my office. A few short steps and I arrive! It's a short commute. No drive-thru breakfasts, parking lot freeways, traffic lights, or the hassle of finding a parking spot. No tolls to pay. Just a few steps from the breakfast nook to my office nook. The workday has begun!

Working from home! What an amazing concept. Virtual work is the norm across the nation. Covid demanded us to be home—cook our meals, play games with our kids, and earn our living from home. Soon, all offices allowed their employees the luxury of not leaving the house! Zoom calls bombarded our living rooms, dining rooms and bedrooms. We worked from home and loved it. Surveys indicate that the productivity level only increased during this time. Virtual work became a booming industry. Agencies across the country were founded to contract virtual executive assistance, virtual personal assistance, virtual bookkeepers, virtual web designers and the list goes on. I jumped on the bandwagon.

I applied to a virtual executive/personal assistance employer. After many aptitude tests, screenings, and several webinars, I was hired as an independent contractor. Currently, I still have engagements with this agency as well as clients under my own LLC. I work for several clients from my home. I can go for walks, go swimming, go on a beach walk, write, or sit outside and read the paper at any time of the day. I can travel any time I want. Just pack up your computer and you can work from anywhere. It's a luxury I cherish. I can opt in for 30-110 hours/month contract work. Sound appealing? I have found out how to make this work for you too!

Allow me to share with you the tips and tactics to prosper and enjoy virtual working! Success in this capacity is based on how you manage your day. When you worked outside of your home, you had a routine. You are now ready to establish a new way of working!

First, there are basic rules to make this the best job ever!

- ❖ Set your alarm the same time you would for an 8:00 a.m. office workday.

- ❖ Get ready for work! Put the coffee on, shower, dress, and prep for the day.

- ❖ Your commute is a few steps away!

- ❖ Depending on your client's time zone, you can adjust your own schedule.

- ❖ Be sure to take breaks, especially fresh-air breaks.

- ❖ Set your alarm for break time. I set my alarm for mid-morning coffee break, 1:00 p.m. lunch/walk a few miles break and a 3 p.m. "get outside" break. It works!

❖ Shut down for the day as you would if you were working in the office. Log off, shut down, put all paperwork away, neatly arrange your desk and "to do" list of the next day, and leave the area!

There are some important guidelines that need to be held with virtual work. These are totally different from office work. If you do not adhere to these guidelines, you will find stress and chaos entering your life, and that is not what we are looking for ever again!

❖ Boundaries. Just as in the office, you need to set boundaries. Your time is valuable. Even though you are not showing up at 8 a.m. and leaving at 5 p.m., you need to create your own start and finish time. It's easy to get up early and start working and continue throughout the day and evening. Burnout is around the corner. It's very easy to look at your computer on Saturday morning and go through emails, etc. Unless you are working on a project with a time-sensitive deadline, you must NOT do this. Otherwise, you will be working 24/7.

❖ Communication. You and your client must be on the same page. If you are an independent contractor, take the lead. Depending on the client's needs and time zone, adjust your workday accordingly. If you are required to be on a 6 p.m. Zoom call, take that into consideration when you plan your day's work. Otherwise, you will be working around the clock. You need to let the employer or client know your intentions for the work week. That is vital to success.

❖ Be respectful of your time. Do not overload your day. Use discretion when choosing the position. Choose out of passion, not just the compensation. The money will manifest when you are doing what you love. Choose clients that spark your interest. Be realistic. Do not take on more than you can handle.

❖ Organization. If you have several clients, or an employer with several projects you are working with, be sure your space is organized. Working from home sometimes leads to smaller spaces. My office is in the corner of my sunroom. I love the openness and windows. However, it is a small area. I utilize every space. I love to color-code, so each client has a distinct color—from notebooks, file folders to post-it notes. Keep it simple and organized. And, at the end of the day, clean off your workspace. Put all notebooks and papers away. Keep it clean and neat. Your mind will work the same.

Virtual work is a joy! As an independent contractor, I have the freedom to select my hours, my clients, and the type of work I enjoy. Passion plays a huge role in the selection of clients. Choose a client you are in alignment with. Someone you respect and are like-minded. Know you can assist them with their needs. If your intuition is telling you otherwise, listen to it. You must also enjoy the work they do. You will be representing them in your work, and if you are not interested or feel it is boring, you will be miserable, and they will be frustrated. Listen to yourself. Take the lead. You are the leader, the CEO, the President of your Virtual World.

Like any other job, organization is key to success! I love to color code each client. Each client has a certain color notebook, files, highlighters, etc. I organize my desk and all my files at the end of each day. Just like when I worked in the office, I keep a running list of things that pop into my mind over the weekend, especially those 3 a.m. wake-up thoughts, near me so I can jot them down and not go into my "office." Your workspace at home is your "office." It is not the space for kids to play, others to hang out, or for you to just sit there and get absorbed into the Google world. Keep it professional, clean and don't forget to put your favorite little object or framed picture on your desk. Just like you did in the office! I have shells, and heart-shaped glass paperweights, along with a daily inspirational quote, which becomes my mantra for the day!

Love what you do, and the money will flow! Again, the Law of Attraction. Allow your future dreams to become your reality—without stress and chaos! You deserve it and are so ready! If Virtual Assistance interests you and the concept is alluring—check it out! Examine what is standing in your way of your dreams?

If you are an employer or an independent contractor and know you do need some assistance, reach out to a Virtual Assistant company and inquire. Your world will change in a positive way! You do not need to interview, process payroll, process a background check, etc. All of the HR duties in hiring are done by the VA company. They will select a candidate that will match your needs, your personality, and your company's business. The outcome is definitely a WIN!

Treasure Chest Gem: The Sunstone

This gem holds personal freedom, and power. It reflects the qualities of solar light-openness, clarity, and consciousness. Virtual work reflects your personal freedom. It is truly a gift to some. If this finds you pondering the idea, I sincerely encourage you to follow your intuition. My hope is that this chapter inspired you to take the leap of faith . . . at any age!

Grazia!

Thank you to all who inspired me to write this book. The idea was formed years ago, and little by little, I was able to put all my thoughts and experiences to paper. Some chapters made me cry, some made me laugh—all were therapeutic. I am grateful for each "character" in this book, the lasting relationships created, the crazy adventures, the laughter, the tears, and the lessons learned as I followed the path that was divinely set before me. I am grateful for the flowing prosperity, and the magnificent, unexpected travels the universe provided.

And, most importantly, I am humbled to share my story.

The best is yet to come,
Mary Ann Gamble

About The Author

After many years of executive/personal assistance in the corporate world, I continue my passion in the virtual world.

My clients are of the same high-profile, C-suite executives with the exact personalities and traits mentioned in the chapters of this book. The only difference from the pages of this book to today, is me! I am older, wiser, and ready to share my stories, tips, and tactics with you!

Today, I both work and live in my sweet, beach bungalow on a quiet, casual, peaceful island.